Best Vegan Science Fiction & Fantasy

2018

Also from Metaphorosis Books

Score – an SFF symphony

Reading 5X5: Readers' Edition
Reading 5X5: Writers' Edition

Best Vegan Science Fiction & Fantasy
Best Vegan SFF of 2018
Best Vegan SFF of 2017
Best Vegan SFF of 2016

Metaphorosis Magazine
Metaphorosis: Best of 2018
Metaphorosis: Best of 2017
Metaphorosis: Best of 2016

Metaphorosis 2018: The Complete Stories
Metaphorosis 2017: The Complete Stories
Metaphorosis 2016: Nearly Complete Stories

Monthly issues

by B. Morris Allen
Susurrus
Allenthology: Volume I
Tocsin: and other stories
Start with Stones: collected stories
Metaphorosis: a collection of stories

Best Vegan Science Fiction & Fantasy

2018

edited by
B. Morris Allen

ISBN: 978-1-64076-003-5 (e-book)
ISBN: 978-1-64076-004-2 (paperback)

from
Metaphorosis Publishing

Neskowin

Contents

From the Editor

I've been spending time lately in Mexico City and in Lima, Peru. Neither is what I would have considered a bastion of veganism. Sure, beans, rice, potatoes, quinoa, etc., but also lots of meat, generally speaking. If that's what you think, you're as wrong as I was. It turns out both are havens for great vegan food ranging from hole-in-the-wall greasy spoon to fancy and sophisticated. And these aren't just outsider imports – spaghetti, pad thai, channa masala – but vegan versions of traditional foods. I've had pistachio-filled soft tacos, jackfruit-layered tortas, cau cau, and a delightful thing called quinotto – a risotto made with quinoa.

So what, you ask? This isn't a cookbook; where are the stories? We'll get there. The point is, from Serbia to Lima, veganism is turning up in unexpected places these day. It's getting so I can't keep up with all the new vegan products anymore. Sometimes they're labeled 'plant-based', but they're vegan all the same.

The SFF community is broadly progressive, and there are writers of all types proclaiming themselves personally, and bringing more diversity into their stories. It's been great to see. I'm disappointed, though to see how few writers are willing to claim the vegan label. They're out there, but somehow 'vegan' has become a term of disparagement – with a tone that the SFF world just wouldn't take against most other minorities.

That's part of why these anthologies exist – to claim back veganism and say there's a lot about it to be proud of. Also, of course, to just assemble a whole bunch of vegan-friendly fiction. That's what we've done here. I have no idea about these authors' personal philosophies; I haven't asked, and don't find it important. What *is* important is that they're good writers, and these are good stories – that just happen to be vegan-friendly.

With that, go on and enjoy them!

Morris Allen
Editor
1 May 2019

Always Dawn to Forever Night

Luke Elliott

Pwela woke to a chill unknown in the Forest of Always Dawn. Tar and peat filled the air, undercutting the perpetual crispness. She shot to her bare feet.

While she slept, the Rot Thing had stolen her warmstone.

Her warmstone sustained her, let her live in the everglow of the forest. Her palms went slick and her breath came short and shallow. She should flee. Run as far and fast as skylight arcing over a cloud. She should, but she would not. She hated the Rot Thing. It had brought unwelcome change to the Continuance.

She could not allow it. She would reclaim her warmstone.

Pwela found Loper resting in a glade of white heather and woke him with a whistle.

"What is it?" he said, jaws cracking with his yawn. The bogcat stretched his long black body, first his back legs, then his front. Extended claws raked the heather, upturning black loam, and a long tail swished high in the air.

"The Rot Thing stole my warmstone."

Loper hissed.

"You smell it, too. Tar and peat." She scratched behind one of his long, feathered ears in the way he liked. She laid her head against his neck, his ghost-striped fur smooth against her bare scalp. "Will you take me after it?"

"Only since it's you asking," he said.

Such a softie. She climbed onto his back, settling between bony spines.

Loper carried her through the Forest of Always Dawn. The orange of the low-roosting sun lit the leaves in its unending glow, dappling the forest floor. Loper darted into the underbrush, then leapt out onto a fir. Long claws sank into its mossy trunk as he bounded off, clearing a sinkhole full of vine snarls. Pwela held fast to the mane of black hair around his neck, her skin blending against his fur. The harmony of their colors was music.

She laughed as they soared, eyes leaking.

Another leap took them into the heart of a familiar glen. But where baby's breath once flourished white and pink, stains now colored flowers with yellow and brown. Wilting from the Rot Thing's passing.

"What is it?" she asked. But she knew.

Loper bent to chew the grass, then spat with a hacking cough. He growled, a rumbly sound from deep within his chest. "Wrongness stains our forest, Pwela."

She sat tall on Loper's back. "The Rot Thing carries stain and wilt and canker. We must drive it out."

"Do you know the Rot Thing?" her friend asked, voice a near-whisper.

She had never met it, but found she did know. "I have long dreamt of it." A shiver shook her small frame.

"As have I," Loper said.

Together, they followed a trail of wrongness in pursuit of the Rot Thing. The thick underbrush and wide trees of the Forest of Always Dawn thinned and lapsed away. Lessening was the way of borders, but swathes of ugly wrongness marred the gentle margins. It hurt her chest to see beauty so wronged.

And so they crossed into the Desert of Only Day. The sun shone savage above, its radiance afire atop the sands.

"The Rot Thing walks the desert," said Loper. "I smell its wrongness, tar and peat." He climbed a dune slowly, paws sinking.

"Shall I walk?"

"The sand is fire, Pwela. Your softness would not long last it." The heat already lashed against her scalp. Oddly, though, a chill remained in her belly.

"You are kind to worry." She let one hand free of his mane to scratch at a long, feathered ear. "But if you tire, my softness will manage." Bogcats were not of the desert. They came from the deep Moor of Forever Night, where they hunted through chill and gloom. Loper had only come to live in the Forest of Always Dawn to be with her, though he grew to love it.

Loper plodded on, persisting against his disharmony with the desert. If he could endure such extremes, she too could reach the gateway, where surely the Rot Thing headed. Its path was no mystery to her, she realized, and that unsettled her stomach. Perhaps she would even discover what lay beyond the gate. Thoughts of what lay beyond filled her with anxiety, a shrill thing. It made her all out of tune.

◌

An immense dune rose above the rolling sands, so tall it brushed the sun. Its sands quivered and roiled.

"What is it?" she said, gasping.

Loper paused. His back hair bristled against her skin. "Come out," he yelled. The bogcat stepped closer to the dune, growling. His ropy muscles coiled beneath her thighs. "You who lurk beneath the sands, come topside."

The dune rippled, and two long eyestalks burst skyward. Each eyestalk reached higher than Pwela would if she stood on Loper's back. Black orbs swelled at their ends.

A voice like an avalanche shook beneath them. "How dare you tread upon our sands, bogcat? And with that wretched manthing clinging to your fur?"

"I tread where I wish, prawn," said proud Loper.

The eyestalks rose higher and an immense horned shell clove the sands. Chitinous legs tipped with forked pincers lifted a carapace half out. Thick antennae whipped the sands, sending Loper back on his haunches. Fetid winds eddied around the creature.

Pwela stifled a gasp.

"We are not prawn." The voice fell over them.

The dune devil was the largest she'd ever seen, perhaps the largest in all the Continuance.

"I am this bogcat's friend, Old One," Pwela said. "Forgive him, please. He can be thorny for a feline."

"Why does the manthing make words at us?"

Loper growled, prowling the sands.

"I am Pwela. I would be your friend as well."

The dune devil's antennae ceased their lashing.

Pwela unslung herself from Loper's back. Her breath hissed at the burning of the desert. The softness of her feet indeed hated the fiery sand. She trudged toward the dune devil, palms raised. "We only seek to cross your dunes and enter the meadow. We chase the Rot Thing."

"Rot Thing?" the old devil demanded. "You are with the Rot Thing?" An enormous claw rose from the sands around Pwela and clamped over her chest. The dune devil drove out her wind. She gasped, fighting for air.

Loper snarled. "Release her, you crusty shrimp."

The dune devil lifted her toward its maw. Hot, dry breath reeking of spoiled fish blasted her from the furnace of the devil's gullet. Arm-like mandibles grasped for her.

"We are not with the Rot Thing," she screamed. "Enemies, enemies!"

The dune devil stopped just shy of biting into her. "We hate the Rot Thing," it said, voice all clacks and clicking. "Look what it did to us." The dune devil rolled onto one side and moved her toward its underbelly. Black stains of ichor marred its orange carapace. The pools spread inky tendrils, even as she watched.

"It's horrible," she said, eyes welling. Dull ache filled her own belly, chilled from within.

The dune devil released her. Before the sands burned her softness, Loper was at her side, head dipped so she could clamber on to his back.

"How do we beat the Rot Thing, old one?" she asked. "How can I save you from its wrongness and destroy it?"

"You cannot," said the dune devil. It quivered, slowly descending back into the sands. "The Rot Thing has always been, though it shifts form."

"I must try," she said, lip thrust out. "I will reclaim my warmstone and not allow wrongness to desolate my Continuance."

"The Continuance is not yours, manthing," said the dune devil. Soon, only its eyestalks remained above the sands. "It is not for belonging. Shared by all and none."

"Once I cast out the Rot Thing, will you heal?" she asked.

"Look to yourself," the dune devil said. Its eyestalks dipped beneath the sands, which stilled as if nothing had ever lurked beneath its shifting layers.

"We must go, Pwela," said Loper. "Even I cannot long withstand the fire." And go they did, across the Desert of Only Day's long reaches, until tufts of sawgrass dotted sand that lapsed into soil. The sun dipped in the crossing, turned purple.

They entered the gentle meadow of the Everdusk.

Though Pwela was most comfortable in the Forest of Always Dawn, she adored the Everdusk. She and Loper had come once before, played on beds of lilac, rolled together beneath the tranquil light. The autumn wind blew songs of sleepiness and slow. The meadow was a place for resting.

But wrongness had come to the Everdusk, too. The lilac sea had wilted, petal clusters browned and decayed. A sign of the Rot Thing's passing.

The path wound down into the moor and out of sight. Her feet tried to follow, but she forced them to halt. She felt the end in her belly, and rested her palm over the chill. The path led, eventually, to the gate.

"What ails you?" Loper asked.

"A chill," Pwela said, peering at her stomach. She gasped. Wrongness marred her as well, spread from her belly in tendrils of sick.

Loper could not see her belly, since she still rode astride his back. "What is it?" he asked.

"I need my warmstone," she said. "The chill runs deep now, and I cannot shake it." She would spare him the truth.

"We should turn back," said Loper. His black paws sank into the wilted sea. "Please, Pwela. No joy or beauty lies ahead."

"I must face it," she whispered. "It has my warmstone, and without it I cannot stay here. You can go back. Return to the Forest of Always Dawn and run among the elm and fir."

"No." Loper flattened his long ears. "I shall carry you all the way."

She scratched those ears while they walked the lilac sea, which shimmered with light and wind, but soon, far too soon, the meadow, too, began to lapse. The purple glow darkened, deepened, until only black remained. A crescent moon hung alone in the sky at the edge of the Moor of Forever Night, shining pale like milk, white like bone. The dying lilacs turned to weeds and snarls and damp.

She had never been so far.

The blackness of Forever Night had haunted her dreams as long as she could remember, beckoning her.

It had been the Rot Thing all along, she realized, summoning her to the gate.

Loper sloshed through puddles as dark as his fur, between the shadows of cypress trees like grasping ghouls. The moor was his home, she reminded herself. Bogcats lived in harmony with the darkness at the heart of the Continuance, prowled the paths surrounding the gateway. Loper would protect her.

The swamp stank of tar and peat. Loper raised his head to sniff the air, then bounded forward through the gloom. Eyes glinted back through shadow, reflecting moonlight. Loper did not slow, for his eyes glinted too, and the unseen things did not assail them.

They emerged, at last, onto the bank of a still lake lit only by the crescent moon which dipped low over the water, as if reaching for its own reflection. At the middle of the lake rose an island of pale sand. At its center lay the freestanding gateway, plain and brown, locked and bolted.

As it should be.

But beside it stood a figure dark beyond mere black. It stung her eyes like an inverse sun. The Rot Thing. On the island, the Rot Thing extended white hands holding a shape red and luminous, light stark against its depth of black.

Her warmstone.

The Rot Thing lifted the red rock high and brought it down upon the gateway with a crack that thundered over the still lake, raising low ripples. The gate shook and shuddered.

Loper whimpered. "Turn back, Pwela. I cannot swim."

She climbed off his back. "I know. But you have carried me far. And I *can* swim. Stay here, my friend. I will face it alone. Someone must." Her heart told her so. "Let it be me."

"I... understand." Loper said, dipping his wide head. "Our moments in the forest live eternal, though we've passed them by. I am with you, whether you sense me or not. And if you return, I will find you again on the shore."

Pwela hugged his neck, eyes leaking, then dove into the still waters, breaking them, casting waves across the lake. Cold beyond ice bit her everywhere, though not as cold as the wrongness in her belly, but soon the pain of the chill lapsed too. She swam, arm over arm, legs pumping. She laughed as she sped toward the island, laughed despite it all. The song of the water played in her heart, filling her. When she reached the island, she climbed out, cold and dripping, but full of harmony.

"Let the gateway be," she commanded. "It must remain shut."

The Rot Thing stood with its back to her, hood drawn, looming over the gateway, its huge umbral mass shifting and fluid. It smashed the warmstone against the gateway again with a thunder that forced Pwela to cover her ears. Her red rock broke. The gateway's frame cracked, and the Rot Thing turned, then dropped the shining shards of her warmstone to the pale sand. It returned its long hands to its sides.

"No!" she cried. She dropped to her knees and cupped the fragments. Their light faded and was gone.

She dropped the broken bits and glared at the Rot Thing. Her eyes stung from gazing upon shadow so deep, but they soon adjusted too, even to blinding oblivion. She did not look away.

"You do not belong," she said. "Leave this place and never return."

"None belong. All belong," it said, throwing back its hood. "Look within and know you brought me here." The Rot Thing's voice came as a hollow echo of her own, rebounding from an endless cavern. The head of the Rot Thing was her own bald head, but distorted and immense. Chill radiated from it, sapping her strength.

She wanted to scream, to run as far and fast as skylight. She should flee, but she did not.

"You cannot trick me, bastard," she said, rising from the sand. "I did not bring you. You are *not* welcome here. Leave this place!" She set her feet wide and lifted her fists.

"There is only one way." It laid a thin hand against the gateway. "Join me." The Rot Thing's immense face was like her own, but wrongness filled empty eyes above lips blue and frigid.

The gateway opened, and nothing lay beyond. An abyss with no color at all.

She should have never come. The Forest of Always Dawn waited still. Stained though it was, at least it held warmth and sun.

A place for beginnings, not ends.

But no, the wrongness had spread through the heather, through the fir and lilac. To herself.

The Rot Thing held out its hand to her, fingers like white worms.

She searched the far bank for Loper, but the bogcat had gone. It did not anger her. Such things were not easy to witness.

The Rot Thing waited, hand extended.

"I will not go with you," she said, but did not shrink away from the awful hand.

"You will," it said, voice still a hollow echo of her own. "I will not tell you to be unafraid. I will not barter or beg. But you will come."

She stared at the nothing beyond the gate. "What is it? Is there something farther in I cannot see?"

The Rot Thing stood silent, spindle fingers swaying before her. The only way to know was to step through.

She thought of the wilted heather, the browning lilac, the wheezing old dune devil. Loper, so worried for her softness, who had carried her over fire.

"Will you leave the Continuance if I go with you?" she said.

It paused, silent for a time before responding. "I came for you."

Then it was right. "I'm sorry, Loper," she whispered.

She took its hand. Her tiny fingers stuck to the Rot Thing's pallid skin as if it were tar. Near translucent skin. She gasped as black eels wriggled beneath the thin membrane of its being. They coiled beneath her hand, drawn to her warmth.

The crescent moon rent and tumbled from the black. The still lake spilled skyward, rising in a geyser around her.

With one long hand, the Rot Thing pushed through the absence of the gateway and pulled her through with the other, away from the Continuance. She could not stay, only go. And go, she did. Through and beyond into nowhere.

Luke Elliott's story "Always Dawn to Forever Night" was first published in Metaphorosis *on 2 March 2018.*

About the author

Luke Elliott was born and raised in the suburbs of central Florida, but in his late twenties he travelled across the country with his wife and two dogs to live in Portland, Oregon, where he fell in love with the city and region. He has a B.A. in Creative Writing from the University of Florida and earned an MFA in Writing Popular Fiction from Seton Hill University. He writes mostly science fiction, fantasy, and horror, but will go wherever the inspiration takes him. In August of 2017, he launched the Ink to Film podcast with a filmmaker co-host, where he discusses books and their film adaptations from a writer's point of view. In late 2018, he attended the Viable Paradise writers' workshop. In between writing, podcasting, and occasional gaming, he collects and reviews quality whiskies and is always happy to pour a dram for company.

www.lukeelliottauthor.com, www.inktofilm.com, @luminousluke

Pandora, Rising

George Nikolopoulos

I was working the bellows as Father walked in.

"Hail, Hephaestus," he said. I ignored him and went on with my work.

Zeus tensed. He wasn't used to people ignoring him. Still he didn't comment about it, so I guessed he'd come by to ask for a favor—once again. I was right; but what he asked for surpassed even his usual audacity.

"Hephaestus, I'd like you to create a woman for me," he said.

He'd been unfaithful to Mother so many times, with goddesses, nymphs, dryads, you name it. Now he wanted *me* to make a woman for him?

He stood on my left side and my hammer was on my right. I could turn and smite him before he had a chance to strike me with his lightning bolt. I thought of the day he'd tossed me out of Olympus, when I was a small child; I've been a cripple ever since.

As always, I did nothing. If I killed him now, the war for succession might even destroy Olympus.

"What do you want the woman for, Zeus?" I asked. "Have you not had enough yet?"

He laughed, well aware that his laughter was bound to irritate me. "You thought I wanted her for myself, Hephaestus? Don't be a fool; you should know I don't need you for that. I want her to give to Men as a present. She'll be the wife of Epimetheus."

This was unexpected. "You're making a present to Epimetheus?" I asked. "I thought you hated him. His brother stole the Fire from Heaven."

"And he was properly punished for his crime," Zeus said. "I don't hold all men responsible. I want this feud to end and such a gift is a great way to end it." He turned to leave. At the entrance of the cave, he turned back. "Anyway," he said, "the Fire was stolen from *your* forge, so you owe me one; if you create this woman for me we're even."

◌

I tore great chunks of lava off the cave walls and I brought them to my anvil. Working with hammer and fire, I shaped a woman out of lava. I made her in the image of Aphrodite, my estranged wife.

When I finished, I kissed the statue and breathed life into it. For a moment, nothing happened; had I overestimated my powers again? Then she opened her eyes and looked at me. She was like Aphrodite in every respect, but her eyes shone like molten fire. One look, and I knew I was lost forever.

◌

All gods and goddesses were present at her Naming ceremony; all but one. Zeus, the King of Olympus, had not deigned to grace us with his presence. So much the better, as far as I was concerned.

I took her by the hand and escorted her to the altar. I smiled at her. She smiled back. "Your name is Pandora," I said, "*the gifted one.*"

One by one, the gods and goddesses brought her gifts. Aphrodite, acting awkward around her spitting image, brought her a diamond necklace and pearl earrings. Athena gave her a wedding gown, blue like the Aegean Sea. Hera presented her with a headdress that looked like an overgrown peacock; I often wonder about mother's taste in adornments. Apollo gave her a flute, carved out of bone. Ares brought her a sword, of all things; Pandora hesitated for a heartbeat, before accepting it with a graceful smile.

Then I heard a grumpy voice coming from the entrance to the temple: "I haven't been invited to the ceremony." Father had finally arrived, carrying a large chest.

"I didn't suppose the King of Olympus would require an invitation," I said.

He smiled, which always seemed ominous. "Never mind," he said, "I've also brought gifts to the one being named." He produced the chest. "A present for her to give to her husband-to-be, to be precise. It will bring him the grace of Heaven." He looked straight at Pandora. "Don't open the chest, girl. You must present it to your husband at the wedding ceremony."

Pandora smiled. I had a foreboding of doom, but I said nothing.

We spent our last night together in my smithy, the place where she was born. On the morrow, she would marry Epimetheus. I hated him, but most of all I hated Zeus for arranging it. Pandora seemed cool about this assignment. It was the reason she'd been born, after all.

After a long silence, she rose. "I nearly forgot the present of Zeus. I'll take it to the carriage myself."

I caught her arm. "Leave the chest behind, Pandora," I said. "Don't give it to your husband. I have a bad feeling about this."

"You're jealous," she said with a laugh.

"I don't trust Zeus," I meant to say, but somehow my tongue slipped and what came out of my mouth was "I love you."

She frowned, and it was like the sun going down on me. "I'm sorry," I said with a bitter smile. "You're the most beautiful woman in the world, and I'm just a lame blacksmith."

Then she smiled, and the sun rose again, sending waves of warmth washing over me. "I love you," she said. I took her in my arms. I tried to kiss her, but she put her hand over my lips. "I love you as my creator," she continued. "Your first kiss gave me life; I shouldn't have another. Epimetheus is my destined husband-to-be. Let's not talk about this anymore."

She didn't leave my arms. When I tried to break free, she held me to her. She put her head on my chest and we stood there, like statues, for the rest of the night.

*

I couldn't bring myself to attend the wedding; I knew I'd feel better sitting alone in my cave and drinking myself to oblivion. However, a sense of obligation—or a sense of self-loathing—made me want to watch. Centuries ago I'd crafted the *othone*, a device that allowed me to observe faraway events without having to leave the warmth of my cave. I'd made it to spy on Aphrodite; now I used it to view the ceremony unseen.

I managed to watch the vows of love. I even made it through their first kiss—barely. I was about to turn off the device in revulsion when I heard her say, "Epimetheus, this is my wedding present to you and all mankind."

Her two bridesmaids brought the chest forward, and she opened it herself.

Out sprung the demons of Tartarus. Famine, with the dead eyes and swollen belly; Death, with the grinning skull and the scythe; Fury, red eyes and sharp talons; Disease, with pox marks and yellowy skin; War, bronze helmet and bloody sword.

ʘ

Epimetheus' men put Pandora in a cell. Come next morning they would burn her on a stake; they'd already found new uses for the stolen fire.

I used my wristbands to project my spirit to her cell. I saw her lying on a straw mattress, at a corner of her dirty cell, her lovely blue dress in tatters. Rage overwhelmed me. She looked up at me, fierce and proud despite her red, swollen eyes.

"I'm coming to free you," I said. "I'll break down the walls of your cell with my hammer, and I'll smite the Men, one by one."

"Please don't. They're not to blame. My foolishness brought a terrible calamity to mankind. I can't make it up to them, so it's only fair I pay the price. I did enough harm already, I don't want to be the cause of a war between Gods and Men."

Anger made me speak sharply to her. "I'm not going to stand by and watch them burn you," I said. "It wasn't your fault, only Zeus was to blame. Tell them he was the one that asked you to bring them the chest, and they'll have to let you go."

She shook her head. "That would be even worse. It would make war inevitable."

"So you're going to sacrifice yourself for Zeus' sake?"

"No, I'm doing it for *everyone's* sake," she said. "I've thought it over and there's no avoiding it. If you love me, please promise me you won't try to save me."

I squirmed and I writhed, but she wouldn't budge. In the end I reluctantly promised, trying to think of ways to free her without breaking my pledge.

Unexpectedly, she smiled. "Don't worry about me," she said. "I was born in a volcano, made of lava. Do you really believe fire can destroy me?"

I stayed all night in her cell, or my spirit did. I couldn't hold her this time, but we lay close to each other and I swear I could feel her breath on my skin, even though seas and mountains lay between us.

In the morning we heard footsteps and she bade me leave. Just before I withdrew, she said, "Hephaestus, I love you with all of my heart. Wait for me in our cave. I promise I'll come back to you and stay with you forever."

I watched as they burned her, and I could do nothing to save her; I was bound by my promise. Columns of smoke rose from the fire and filled the othone. Then the smoke blew off.

I gazed at the scene of the burning, and my fury erupted like a volcano. She hadn't survived the fire, after all; only ashes remained. I grabbed my hammer and got ready to fly down to the Men and destroy them all.

Before I could move, out of the ashes rose a beautiful bird, colored like the rainbow.

The Men called it Hope; hope for the world. The Gods called it the Phoenix. But I knew better. "*Pandora!*" I called, and she took to the skies and flew to me.

George Nikolopoulos' story "Pandora, Rising" was first published
in Galaxy's Edge *Issue 33 on 7 January 2018.*

About the author

George Nikolopoulos is a speculative fiction writer from Athens, Greece, and a member of Codex Writers' Group. His short stories have been published in over 60 magazines and anthologies including *Galaxy's Edge, Nature, Daily Science Fiction, Factor Four, Grievous Angel,* and *The Year's Best Military & Adventure SF.*

All the Colors I Cannot See

L'Erin Ogle

I remember everyone being lit up in colors when I was a little kid. They wore vivid blues and pinks and greens and yellows. Everyone dripped in thoughts and feelings. They were painted with sky blue happy or scarlet red mad, thunderhead gray sad and bright orange excited. I loved looking at everyone wearing their hearts out like that, and mostly everyone had real nice shines. Then I met a man with no color at all.

That's when we lived outside the little town of Misty, which hugs the line of Maximillian and the Southern Triangle, and still ain't decided which one it wants to be a part of. We farmed orchards with apples and oranges and fat bunches of grapes, and Mama had a vegetable garden that spat out vegetables bigger than anyone else's. She can make anything grow big and better tasting just with her hands.

We went to town with Mama sometimes, when she needed seeds or something else that couldn't wait for Daddy to get the next day. We'd walk down the dusty dirt roads, until we got close to the center of town where the roads turned into big flat stones cobbled together.

Every time we went to town, Mama stopped and bought us a lemonade at the corner store. It was so full of sugar it made a little coating on your teeth, that you could lick the rest of day, still taste the sweet. Mama ain't big on sweets, and it was always my favorite part. Carly always sipped hers all the way home, but I swallowed gulp after gulp until my throat seized up and sent needles through my head.

I was five the last time we ever went into Misty. It was real sunny that day, so bright I had to squint to see anything at all. We came on the man with a shiny black hat and matching coat right where the dust turned to stone. Under his hat, his face was pale and the way the sun was steaming off the pavement, it made his face blur, like it was melting right off. I squinted real hard, trying to see what kind of shade he was throwing off, but not a single color came off him.

"Mama," I said and tugged her hand. Me and Carly was on either side of her, our heads right at her waist even though Carly's four years older than me. Daddy says Mama and Carly are pint sized. Not like me and him.

"What?" Mama said, real irritated, pink with it. She got all nervous and twitchy when we came to town.

"That man ain't got no colors," I whispered.

His head turned real smooth and he smiled at me. Not at Mama and Carly, but at me. Underneath his glossy black mustache, his teeth were white and square and too big for his mouth. Looked fake. As we drew near, he bent at the waist like he was taking a bow, and said loud, "Hello, little girl! Would you like to see what I have inside my hat?"

"Yeah!" I said, tugged my hand free of Mama's, ran towards him.

"Grace!" Mama snapped and hustled after me.

The man took his hat off one handed and turned it upside down, passed his free hand over it in circles.

"Grace," Mama said, and I felt her fingers knifing into my shoulder. "Sir, we are late, no time for tricks, excuse us."

"We ain't late," I said. "I want to see."

The man dipped his hand in his hat and pulled out a fat white snake. It made an odd purring sound, and he looked at my Mama and smiled. I reached out and felt scales shiver soft and smooth.

"Come on, Grace," Mama said. She yanked on my shoulder.

The man closed his hand around the snake and dipped it back in his hat, Then he pulled it back out, and when he spread his fingers out there were three golden eggs, the same color as the little bubbles of light that came from Mama when she sang. "Little snakes are most often vulnerable in the egg, just like little birds in the nest," he told us.

"Grace!" Mama said, and this time she pulled harder, and I stumbled backwards, crying out 'cause it hurt. My mad mixed with my hurt feelings and floated away red and orange.

I went with her, my head turned around to look back at the colorless man. He was still smiling away. He kept his eyes on mine and leaned forward and blew a tiny snake from his mouth that landed on the middle egg. It hammered its triangle head into the shell and disappeared with its tail flicking back and forth.

"Turn around, Grace," Mama said, dragged me down the street. She held me so tight that I wore a purple wrist bracelet the next day.

"We never forget magic," the man called after us. "Not the kind that turned its back on its brothers!"

Mama's face got bone white and a real ugly color like wet ash circled her head. We didn't stop again, not for seeds, not even for lemonade.

"Why couldn't we see the magician?" I demanded. I was sparking yellow orange red.

We were on the dust roads leading out of town, and Mama stopped right in the middle of the road. She got down on her knees, looked at me and Carly real serious. Her color was a dark blue, twisted up with orange.

"That man wasn't a magician. He was a snake charmer," she said.

"What's a snake charmer?" Carly asked.

"It's a bad kind of magic," she said. "That's why we don't tell people about Grace seeing colors. Or about the light bubbles when I sing, or that I have the gift of growing. A long time ago, there was magic in a lot of places. But there was our kind of magic, the good kind, and then the dark magic. The snake charmers. Now, they didn't start as all bad. But sometimes they used their power to get things, when it wasn't fair to other people. And then people, the ones with no magic, became angry and scared. So, they chased the people with magic away, wouldn't sell things to them in town, wouldn't allow their children to go to school, that sort of thing. And then even people with good magic started hiding theirs, because they didn't want to get run off. Lots of the snake charmers died off. And the ones that were left, they had so much anger about being driven out, they turned mean as snakes. That's why people started calling them the snake charmers."

And she didn't say nothing else the way home. We got sent to our room so she could have peace and quiet. I heard her tell Daddy about the snake charmer as soon as he got home.

She was all kinds of colors, flashing red and blue and black and gold in pulses. "We can't stay here."

"Julia," Daddy said. "Maybe he was just a magician?"

"He had a snake come out his mouth, and crawl into the eggs the bird laid," I said. I was still supposed to be in my room.

"Grace," Mama said. "Room. Now."

I went to my room and closed the door loud, then tiptoed back out to listen.

"Maybe he's just passing through?" Daddy said. "He won't want people to catch onto him. I bet he's already moved on."

"You don't understand," Mama said. "Charmers hate my kind. He saw me, I know. He heard what Grace said. He'll come, and he won't stop coming until he's dead, maybe not even then, Nate. We have to go. Tonight. We have to run. I mean, I can grow anything. We'll go south where they don't mind a little magic as long as it don't hurt anyone. We make a new home."

There was a time when Daddy did anything Mama wanted. There was more talking but we left Misty that night.

It's funny but as time passed I sort of forgot the whole thing, even the awful bumpy midnight ride down here to South Song. It felt more and more like a dream if it did cross my mind.

✺

First time I said anything about colors here, Mama shook her head. "Grace," she said. "It's time to stop being fanciful. There aren't any colors. It's just your imagination."

"No, it ain't," I said. "You made us move 'cause I didn't see no colors round that man, Mama." "That wasn't why," Mama said.

"But—"

"Grace," Mama said. "Stop arguing with me right now. I don't want to hear another word about colors, or I'll tan your little behind. There aren't any colors."

Bout that time was when Mama seemed to be finding wrong with anything I did. It felt like being slapped, knowing she knew I was telling the truth and she was saying it wasn't so.

I remember being so mad that my eyes stung with it. Ain't nothing worse than trying to say something and being told to shush.

I tried not seeing them. Not talking about them. But two days later I saw a woman with a big belly, when we went to town to get some things. I knew the lady was growing a baby inside her, but I don't get excited about that. What I got excited about was the bright pink web spinning out from her, clear into the sky. It was so damn pretty against the sky I couldn't breathe. "Mama!" I pointed above her head. "Look at the color!"

Mama's lips skinned tight against her teeth, turned pale white. She jerked my hand so hard I almost tripped. "Ssshh," she said, tinted a real ugly maroon.

When we got home, she made good on her hide tanning promise. I lay in bed the rest of the day with my eyes shut. Whenever I opened them, I saw ugliness.

❂

You'd think I'd never have said a damn word about the colors ever again. I didn't talk about them, even to Carly. I tried to ignore them, and they started fading on me. It was tolerable enough, but sometimes I felt all hollowed out inside.

I was eight years old and two days when I seen Brian, a man my daddy's age, doing his limp down the street. He had gotten bucked off a horse a year before and it did something bad to his hip. He got sort of mean after that. He was always stained with a dark red hue if I looked real hard. His daughter Marley went to school with us, a real skinny girl with shiny blond hair. I didn't really know her 'cause she was almost sixteen. But people knew her daddy was bad on the drink, since the accident. People always got something to say about stuff like that.

This afternoon, I couldn't rightly see if he was on the drink, 'cause he was wrapped up in black so dark it looked wet. Like spilled ink all over his paper white skin. He was muttering to himself, too, looked crazy.

I felt ice cold looking at him all messy like that. I crossed the street so we didn't share the same side of the road. I went home and couldn't eat. I kept seeing that ink cloud. It had me wondering if things like that could leave the person they was on and come after other people.

Next day, Marley was just gone. Her mama went door to door, banging away, asking had anyone see Marley. My daddy went to town, to join the men who were going to search for her. I sat at the table and tried to tell Mama, about the ink cloud.

"Mama, I saw Marley's daddy in town yesterday," I said.

"And?"

"And he was walking down the street, and he scared me."

Mama stopped and looked at me. "What did he do?" she asked. "Was he on the drink again?"

"I don't know, ma'am," I said. "But he had real bad color around him like a cloud of real black—"

Mama took in some air, and when she blew it out, it was mad and scared, red and blue gray. "Goddammit, Grace," she whispered. Her eyebrows yanked down and a big fat line appeared in between them. "I have told you, and told you—"

"But Mama—"

"But nothing, Grace!" she roared. "Go to your damn room, right now!"

Mama tanned me again, worse. I stopped crying after the first couple licks, 'cause this mad feeling just sort of took over. *Ain't ever gonna let her see me cry again,* I promised myself. And when she was done, she was one crying. She knelt down beside me and she said, "Grace, this is for your own good. If you keep on talking about colors, people will get bad ideas. You have to forget about Brian, and Marley, and the colors. You hear me? You forget it all."

There's an old saying that there are some things better left forgotten, but that ain't right. There are things you should never forget. I knew I was seeing something important, but even that feeling sort of drifted away, faded like dreams do.

I don't like the new teacher. He smiles to greet us when we file into the big old school room that used to be a barn. It's the only building big enough to fit all of us, from the little kids still wiping snot on their sleeves, up to the older kids who only care about making big dumb moon eyes at each other. When he smiles, one of his lips curls up higher on one side, reveals big square teeth. It tugs at something in my head, but I don't know what. It's like everything faded with the colors.

The colors are little ghosts of their old selves, all faded and barely there. They only show up bright if it's real important. I guess looking at them sort of feels wrong, like peeping into other people's heads. There's some feelings people have that you don't want to see.

But Ellison ain't got no color, note even a hint of it, at all.

"I don't like him," I whisper to Carly.

Carly rolls her eyes. "Shut up and go sit down," she whispers back – "before you get us in trouble."

She shakes her hair as she walks down the side of the rows, like she's getting it behind her shoulders, but she's just doing it so everyone looks at her. She's real proud of all that golden hair she brushes one hundred times every morning and night. She likes being smart, but she likes being pretty more. She about pooped a kitten when she was voted the prettiest girl last year by the boys. They wrote her name on a piece of paper with little stars and hearts drawn around it, and she crowed about that all damn summer.

I didn't even make the pretty girl list, which Carly said was 'cause I was too young. She was being nice for once, but I don't care about that dumb list. You just know the girls who got excited about that are gonna pop out a hundred kids and get stuck right here in this dusty town where nothing ever happens. Me, I'm gonna be the first girl to ride to the North Border and back, just to show everyone I can. I'm gonna make history.

"I'm Mr. Ellison," the man says. Then he tells me, "Put that chair down on all four legs, Grace Milliken."

Then, he makes us change all our seats. We have to sit in the order of youngest to the oldest, which puts me in the front row. Stupid, 'cause I'm four inches taller than everyone in the second row. The front's for suck ups like Carly. I cross my arms and slouch when Ellison walks by, carrying a long, thin wooden pointer. He snaps it down on my leg right above the knee when he passes.

"Sit up straight, Grace Milliken," he says.

I ain't never been hit before by an adult, and I don't like it. It hurts, but worse, everyone saw it happen. I sit up straight and fold my arms across my chest, hot all through my face.

Everyone sits up arrow straight then. Nick's next to me looking out the side of his eyes and shrugging in sympathy. He ain't half bad, for a farmer boy. Ellison gets up to Carly's row, near the back since she's one of the oldest. Carly raises her hand. "Mr. Ellison, sir?"

Here we go. Everyone loves Carly 'cause she's just so *proper* and *perfect*.

"Yes, Carly?"

He already knows all our names on the first damn day. I don't like it, not at all.

"Sir, I can't see the board."

I sneak a look back, see James the 1st directly in front of her. There are two James, and this James is the big one, taller than anybody in class. Being short like she is, Carly can't probably see anything but the dirt on his neck. I snicker inside. Even if she can see, James the 1st's daddy has a hog farm and he's always stinking to high hell.

Mr. Ellison sighs. His noises are louder than his words. He's that kind of person.

I'm really lookin at him, how even the color around him looks faded. I want to tell someone, but I can't. Not anymore.

For being magic, Mama sure hates it. She can grow things just by touching them. When she sings, little bubbles of light float around her, but she pretends not to see them. My seeing colors ain't as good, 'cause I'm half ordinary like Daddy, but it's mine all the same. Carly can't do a lick of magic, but she's perfect in every other way. Everyone thinks so, except maybe Ellison, 'cause he just sighed at her.

That sigh Ellison makes, I see it hanging above Carly, see through but it's thicker than the rest of the air. I sit up a little, 'cause I ain't never seen that before.

"Are you saying I've made a poor choice, Carly, with my seating arrangements?" He smiles, his stupid lip curling up.

Carly flushes like I did. There ain't no right way to answer his question, and we all sort of wait to see what happens in the worst kind of quiet.

"No, sir, I was just- "

"Just what?" he slices into her mid-sentence. His eyes are squinted slits.

No one ever talks to Carly like that. She bites her lip, looking around, and I damn near feel sorry for her, but not sorry enough to stop thinking it was about time. *A little humility's good for the spirit,* Daddy said, the first time I fell off a horse and cried like a girl. *Makes you realize you ain't perfect.*

"No, sir," Carly whispers. She's staring at her hands in her lap. Her hair falls around her face. She's real pretty, like Mama. She's got little bones and big eyes, and big masses of long golden hair. Me, I'm tall and big through the shoulders like Daddy. Colored all different browns and tans, eyes and hair, average. I got robbed on that 'cause his good looks don't translate to my face.

"Are we going to have a problem this semester, Carly?"

He should let her alone after that, but he don't. He ain't smiling on the outside, but I think he is on the inside.

"No," she says, real soft.

"Stay when I dismiss the others," he says, and moves past her.

Carly's crying.

I feel bad, honest, but she's always been a crier.

⟡

I forget my lunchbox on purpose. I want to hear what that big galoot has to say to my sister. Just 'cause I don't always like her don't mean I stop looking out for her. If she's got a fault, it's that she'll believe any damn thing people tell her. Three years she spent a whole week eating only potatoes when I told her they'd make her skin glitter. I heard it from this girl who had real pretty skin, said a boy up north wrote a song about it.

Or so she claimed. Me, I don't go around just believing any damn thing people say.

Carly's got her nose to the corner. I can see just the side of her face. Her cheek has old dusty tracks from the crying before. Ellison stands just a step away, no expression at all on his face. He's talking real intense, right in her ear. His words come out little colored snakes of yellow and green that slither into her ear. I strain my ears trying to catch what he says, but all I hear is hissing. The hissing is making me sick, like I might puke so hard breakfast comes out my nose. I feel hot and dizzy, so I get outside, where everyone's still sitting and eating. It can't have been long I was gone, but it felt like damn near forever.

Carly don't come out until I'm finishing my sandwich, trying to help my stomach stop turning flips.

She don't look no worse for the wear now, and don't stop to talk to me, so I mind my own business.

○

I don't say nothing about the snakes and Ellison to anyone. I'll just get tanned for it and no one will believe me anyway.

○

Carly nibbles at dinner and goes straight up to bed. When I get up to our room, she's standing there in her drawers, pinching at her stomach. She must have been doing it for a while, 'cause there are red blotches all along the top of her waist.

"What the hell you doing?" I ask.

"Don't curse, Grace," she says. She turns her head, looks at the back of her thigh. I see pinch marks there too. "I'm getting fat."

I snort. "You're real skinny. You're practically a walking skeleton. Why the hell would you think that, and why the hell you pinching yourself? Ain't nothing there but skin, and you're going stretch it all out doing that."

"You ought to start talking right," she says. "Otherwise people will think you're stupid. Anyway, it was just something someone said. Just forget it."

I go to bed thinking about how everyone always wants me to forget.

○

What do you think of the new teacher?" Dad asks at dinner next day.

"Hate him," I say.

"Grace!" Mama says. "Don't use that word."

"Well, what am I supposed to say? I do." I stab my fork into my potato, which splits down the middle. Me and Carly love potatoes. We both put a big fat pat of butter inside them and let it melt into the white stuff. "Pass me the butter, Carly."

"Strongly dislike," Mama says.

Carly pushes the butter plate over without taking any. She starts cutting her potato into tiny pieces. She puts one in her mouth and chews slowly.

"Not hungry?" Dad asks Carly.

"Well, someone at school told Carly she's fat, so she ain't eating," I say.

Mama frowns and Dad puts his fork down. "Who the hell called you fat?" Dad says.

"Well, where does Grace get it from, now?" Mama says to Dad, but it's just a reflex. She looks at Carly. "Carly, is that true?"

"No," Carly says. I see color in that lie, dirt brown, like shit. It's the first time in a couple years I seen a color that ain't all faded like old clothes and the first time I ever heard Carly lie.

"That's a goddamn lie!" I say real loud. I'm mad as hell. I can feel a whole bunch of things twisting around in my chest, wanting to come out.

"Grace!" Mama snaps, and this time I see her face beet red. I don't need to see nothing else to tell me she's mad. "You go to your room right now!"

"But she told a damn lie!"

"Get in your room Grace!" It comes out as dull red pulses. Seems like whenever Mama's got color, it's always at me, and it ain't never a nice color.

"This ain't fair, she doesn't even want to eat!" I holler, and stomp upstairs.

Dad comes up after a while. I paced around at first, but now I'm lying on my bed, still steaming. The bed dips when he sits down, rocks back and forth. He's a big, solid man. When he wraps his arms around Mama she practically disappears. "Hey kiddo," he says. "You know you can't curse like that."

"But she lied! You'd be pissed if someone lied on you too!" I glare at him.

"You sound just like your mama, you know. She was always getting all hot and bothered about something and getting herself in trouble."

"I don't believe you," I keep my face buried in the pillow. "Bet she was perfect, just like Carly's lying butt."

He laughs real low, says, "Aw, Grace, no one's perfect."

He pats me on the head and tells me to come finish dinner. I drag my feet on the stairs so everyone knows I'm still in my feelings about what happened. Mama's cleaning up and Carly's sitting at the table, most of her plate in front of her. I sit down and glare at her.

"Eat, Grace," Mama says without turning her head. Sometimes she knows what I'm doing without even looking. "And Carly, you're not done until you finish your plate."

I finish first, and get sent right back upstairs, which gets me mad all over again. Carly doesn't come up until it's dark, bedtime.

"You finally eat?" I snap at her, ready to fight.

"No," she says. She goes to bed without even brushing her hair. I lay there and look at my breath, steaming out maroon. It takes me a while to settle down, get to sleep.

○

I'm seeing colors again a lot. I don't like it.

○

Next day, Carly says she's sick and won't get out of bed. I go out with Mama and Dad and prune trees in the orchard, and then we all come in and play a game of cards. If I could see my colors now, I know they'd be all sky blue right now. I like it being the three of us sometimes.

*

"You giving up on your good looks?" I ask Carly, walking to school. She only brushed her hair a couple times this morning and didn't pinch her cheeks or run her finger through the jam and paste it to her lips either. "You ain't hardly brushed your hair."

"Why should I?" Carly says. She's walking with her head tilted to the side, like I do when I get water in my ear. "No one cares what my hair looks like when I'm this fat."

She's skinny as ever. "You ain't fat," I tell her.

"They say I am," she says, still walking with her head craned almost to her shoulder.

"Who? What the hell is the matter with you?" I like the way that sounds coming out. Dad says that to Mama when she gives him a hard time about his ales at night. A sharp-edged joke.

"Do you hear that?" Carly says instead of answering.

"Hear what?"

"The birds," she says. She stops and turns in a circle real slow. "Their wings. The talking."

"What birds?" The road we walk to school on is bare of trees, just a dusty stretch of road leading to a dead end.

"They're everywhere," she whispers. "In here." She taps her head. I see color starting to appear around her. She's the color of fireplace ashes and embers.

I don't know what to do or say. After a minute she just walks on.

I trail behind her, inspecting the sky for anything with wings.

○

Day 4, Carly don't spell wicked right, leaves the c out. Ellison keeps her in for recess. I sneak in but he isn't hissing this time. Instead, Carly sits at her desk, every part of her bowed over. He sits at his desk, with his fingers steepled together. His smile a mean curve to his face, and all the color in the room is gone. Not just from him but gone from the walls and books and plants.

○

"Something's wrong at school," I tell Dad. He's started in on the dead orchard trees lying in pieces behind the orchard. He strips them of their bark, sands them down, makes things. He don't never know what he's gonna do until it takes its own shape. He says things want to be made.

"Bad wrong?" he asks.

Dad asks one question, and listens. Mama asks a hundred and don't.

"Yeah," I say. "It's Ellison. He hates Carly. He keeps her inside for lunch all the time and I think he says mean things to her."

"Mean things like what?" Dad stops and rests his hands on the tree between his legs.

"I don't rightly know the exact words," I tell him. "I just know he does."

"She tells you that?"

"I went back inside for my lunch first day," I say. "He was in her ear, talking real quiet."

"He yell? Or put his hands on her?"

"No, sir," I say.

"But it made you scared? Or scared for Carly?"

"Made me mad, but made me fearful, sir."

"Gracie," he says. He put his hands on his hips. "Did he tell Carly she was fat?"

"I don't rightly know," I say. I hesitate, try to think how to explain it the thing I can't explain. "He's not a good person, Daddy. I can tell, you know I can. I think he's bad. Real bad."

"Gracie," he put his hand on my shoulder. "I believe you. You know why?"

"Why?"

"You ain't said a damn swear word this whole time," he says. He smiles, but he has to work at it. "I'll take care of it, kiddo. Alright?"

"Yes, sir," I nod. I get a bad feeling, but I don't know why. It's sort of like I know I got a big boulder rolling, but I don't know where it's going. I don't feel like talking anymore, and I turn to leave.

"Gracie?" Dad says. "You see any colors round him?"

We don't talk about the colors since Mama said not to.

"If I see them, they're not good ones," I say, but I don't wait to see his reaction. He wants to talk about colors if it was about Carly. That sort of sticks somewhere in me, but I ain't going to tell anyone about it.

۞

"What the hell did you say?" Carly comes at me, and I'm faster than her but the cursing froze me. Violet clouds erupt from her nostrils and scatter. It scares me, what I'm seeing.

"Hell!" I throw up my arms to protect my face, but she don't swing, pushes me down on my bed instead. My head hits the wall, and I push back at her. "What the *goddamn hell*, Carly?"

"You tell Dad or Mama?" she snaps.

"Tell 'em what?"

"About me getting in trouble at school." Her eyes are jumping out of her head, crazy like her hair's getting.

"I didn't say nothing about you getting in trouble," I say. "I said that damn Ellison is mean to you."

"That's getting in trouble!" Carly says. Big fat tears start slipping out of her eyes. "I ain't nothing but trouble!"

"That's a goddamn stupid thing to say," I tell her. "Ellison say that?"

She glares at me. "He doesn't say a goddamn thing to me, understand?"

"Liar," I whisper.

She pushes me again, and this time my head cracks the wall good. All my air gusts out and I ain't even mad. She's lost her damn mind. I want to get good and mad, but I'm sort of scared to. I ain't never seen someone shoot sparks from inside like she is.

"You just mind you own business," she said, up so close her words lash my face. "You little spoiled *bitch*."

I don't say nothing after that. Don't change into my bedclothes either. I just crawl under my sheets, pull them to my neck, and stare at the ceiling wishing I could make pretty colors that flowed and painted over the bad ones. It's a long time before I close my eyes.

◌

Carly don't say a word to me walking to school. She walks the whole time with her head tilted, frowning. A kaleidoscope of darkness spinning webs from her. I wish the colors would go away.

◌

Daddy comes walking into school just before lunch. Ellison sees him but don't stop talking about the old Gods. Yesterday he said how the old Gods abandoned their people, left them with special powers that the people from before didn't like. How the people decided they would get rid of people who were different, how they drove them off and murdered them and stole their children. Beat anything different right out of them. But he said there was something called full circle which meant that what goes around comes around. He drew on the chalkboard a snake in a circle eating its own tails.

But today he talks about the same stuff our other teachers did. About history, how often people used to worship their Gods, how some of them still have old paintings and books they read out of every day, blah blah blah.

Daddy leans up against the wall against the back of the classroom, his arms folded across his chest, listening. I sneak a look back at Carly, who's either so mad she erased it off her face, or scared. I can't tell but I feel smooth as a turquoise sea, 'cause my Daddy's a man takes care of things.

Ellison dismisses us and walks right up to Daddy, extends his hand. They shake hands, but Daddy takes a minute to do it. He holds that slimy hand, half the size of his, and they look each other up and down.

"Mr. Milliken, I presume?" Ellison nods at me, waiting. "Your daughter is a fierce likeness."

"In more ways than one," Daddy says. He let go of Ellison, looks at me. "Go on outside, Gracie. You too, Carly."

Ellison's lips skim his teeth, peel back. Both sides, but I look real close at his mouth and see the side that usually curls up twitching away under his skin.

I hate waiting. When Daddy strides out, he don't seem no different. He says goodbye to Carly, kisses her on top of the head, then pulls me alongside him. He keeps his voice real low when he speaks.

"That man," he says, just to me. "or any other, for that matter, is not to keep you or Carly at lunch or after school, ever, by yourselves. You hear me? He tries to, you come right home and get me. You understand Gracie?"

"Yes, sir," I say.

"Now go on," he says. "I'll be here to walk you girls home."

I go in feeling smug, like I won, and then I see little tendrils of smoke coming off Ellison. He's thick with them, and I feel more scared than mad just like that. All his face is tight, like it's being sucked in, cheekbones knives ready to slice through the flesh and let the real him out.

He's a man with no color. He's a snake charmer. I guess I knew it, sort of. You know how you know something, but you ain't ready to believe it? Like maybe your Mama likes your sister better, but you just pretend she don't? It's the kind of knowing you pretend ain't there.

Me and Carly get sent right to our room so Mama and Dad can talk. Carly don't want to listen, but I do. I press my ear against the door and I hear them talking real urgent. I wished I could see what their words are wearing, but I'm cutoff from what's happening, and I hate it. I got to tell them about the rest of it, how Ellison's got the black magic. I want to know exactly what is going to happen, so I can rein in this damn fear horse thundering through me.

The sun dips low before they call us down. Mama's pinned her pale hair back and her eyes have gone from bright blue to dark. She's fidgeting like I do at school. Daddy's sitting sideways in his chair, elbow resting on the table.

"I know you two must want to know what's going to happen," Mama says.

"This is so stupid," Carly says, crying. She's got more of a water supply than anybody I know. "Nothing happened."

"Hell, it didn't," Daddy says. His eyes are narrow in his face. He's looking at Carly like he maybe wants to smack her, which I feel in my bones. "I don't know what's been going on down at that school, but you aren't acting right, Carly."

"Ellison, he's a snake charmer," I say. I'm so scared I'm shaking, but I gotta get this out. "I know it. He's like that man we ran away from. He hissed snakes right in her ear!"

"You don't know a damn thing," Carly says. "You think you're so smart, everyone does, but you're *not*."

"We're not arguing," Mama says. "We're not even discussing. Until we get this handled, neither of you are going to school."

"But that's not fair!" Carly bursts out, hollering. "IT'S NOT FAIR!" and she just screams it over and over until it blurs into one long continuous color flashing desperation at us. Then her limbs go boneless and she flops onto the floor, crying. Mama gets down to her knees beside her.

"But it's the only time the birds are quiet," Carly moans.

"What birds?"

"The ones in my head," Carly says. "All day and all night, they beat their wings inside me and I can hear it in words in my head, they're saying the most terrible things, and it only stops there, at school."

Dad and Mama look at each other, over Carly unspooled on the floor. I think they might tell me to go to my room, but I think they forgot me. There's only the three of them—the broken one, and the scared adults.

"What do they say?" Mama asks, real nice. Her voice molasses over pancakes, so sugar sweet it makes my teeth ache. "Carly, darling, tell me what the birds say."

"Fat," Carly whispers. "Ugly. Stupid. Worthless. Good for nothing. They tell me I'll have to be a whore because I can't do anything at all, and I'll be bad at it, because I'm so fat and ugly."

There's a great crack through the room and we all jump. Even Dad himself, who looks at the big seam that now runs down the table. His fingers are white knuckles of rage.

Mama gets Carly calmed down, carries her to their bed. Dad paces. She comes out and she tells me to sleep in their bed with Carly. I tell her no, don't leave me with Carly. I'm whining, near tears.

"You take care of your sister, now, Grace," she says. She kisses me on the top of the head. She looks at me. "I'm awful proud of you, Grace. You're very brave. Like your father."

I go in and lay next to silent Carly, on top of the sheets. Her body curves away from me, a slivered half-moon against the sheets. I lay board stiff next to her, thinking about the whores. I guess I never did think about them before. I know about sex, and stuff. I mean, I'm eleven and I have an older sister who's kissed boys but nothing else. I ain't even sure what a whore is, except it's a woman who does sex type stuff with lots of men.

I know that's how we came from Mama and Dad too. Mama told us the first time Carly asked. *We made you with our bodies*, she said, and thinking about now, in their bed makes me feel hot and uncomfortable. They ain't always quiet about it, but it's always when I'm supposed to be sleeping, so I can't rightly complain. But I feel odd, thinking about it now.

I get up and sit at the edge of the bed. I can hear Mama and Daddy talking about moving away again. Carly has her eyes closed, maybe sleeping. I reach over and brush her hair like Mama did to calm her down. She doesn't stir but then my fingers brush up against something hard.

I tug it out a knot, but it's not hair.

It's a feather.

○

Carly pitches a fit this morning. I wake up when her feet drum the bed and little rat a tat tats run down her spine, which curves unnatural. I scream until Dad and Mama come. Dad freezes statue still, but Mama comes and gathers Carly in her arms. She starts to sing, first just a melody from words I know. Then the song glows and spins. The words stretch and change until I can't recognize them, getting long and dancing around the room, rainbows spinning in little circles.

Carly's body stops shaking and she's limp in Mama's arms.

Dad's moving again, a big tree of a man trembling like a leaf. "Julia," he says. "We should just pack up and go. Right now."

"It's too late," Mama says. "He's already got inside her somehow."

Daddy's twisting his hands together and they're turning red. "What, then?"

Mama looks at him. "It won't stop, Nate."

"Alright," Daddy says. "Alright."

The space between them uncurls and fills with black ink.

Daddy leaves then.

○

Mama and I clean up Carly, starting with her hair. Mama gives me her comb and she takes Dad's and we tease the ends out first. It takes some doing, but with slow small strokes, we get most of the tangles out without cutting it.

"Mama?" I say.

"Gracie?" she makes it a question.

"He did it. Ellison put the birds in her head. The first day. I went back to get my lunch and he was saying something to her, and I could see his words like snakes go right in her ear. I should have told you, huh? You could have fixed it?"

"Oh, Grace," she says. She stops and hugs me right against her.

I'm as tall as her, and wider still, but she still circles me up somehow.

"I wouldn't have listened, probably," she says. "You know? Sometimes I don't listen."

"I know," I say, and she squeezes tighter.

"You haven't hugged me in so long," she murmurs.

"Where's Daddy?" I ask.

Her body goes stiff. She lets go and I don't need colors to tell me she's ashamed and scared and defiant all at the same time. I guess 'cause I feel all them feelings too. I knew it when she told Daddy to go. I seen blackness stretched between them, the kind where there ain't no light at all.

"He went to kill Ellison," I say. I know it's true. I feel a real blackness inside me too, thick and ugly, squeezed up round my heart.

"The connection has to be broken," Mama says. "By any means necessary. You saw Carly this morning. She could die."

"I ain't saying its wrong," I say. "What's Daddy mean? It never ends?"

"You can't make it go away, any kind of magic. It just takes another shape."

"Why though?" I ask. "Why us?"

Right then, Carly sits up. She has half her hair smooth as melted butter and half a huckleberry bush. Her eyes are wide and there ain't nothing in them. She opens her mouth and I think she's gonna scream but birds start spilling out of her mouth. Blackbirds, owls, little gray and red plumed birds, too big for her. They come and come and Mama screams. I don't think but I jump up and run to the big window. I shove it open, catching splinters in all my fingers. The birds beat their wings without stopping, going right through a window way too damn small for their size and number, but it happens.

Outside they caw and beat and their wings make a hard rain sound. It softens as they begin to move farther off.

Carly collapses back on the bed and lies still.

I miss my Daddy so fierce I could die right now.

Mama puts her head down and sobs.

I go to the floor and put my head down and don't.

○

We all pretend things are fine, now.

Dad came home vacant eyed to Carly sitting up, talking. She didn't remember a damn thing. Mama was petting her, the way you do a fresh kitten. I was squeezing my hands together, blind to the fact blood was dripping from all them splinters. Daddy was washing blood off his hands when I felt mine aching, saw the mess I'd made. I sort of gasped, and Daddy saw the splinters. He sat me down and took each splinter out like I might break, and when he was done, he laid his head against the table and sobbed.

We all broke in some way, I guess.

Dad doesn't come home until late now. Sometimes, he smells like other women. Mama and he argue about it, and sometimes they make noise after but it isn't quiet and it isn't nice. Once I very clearly heard Mama say 'hurt me, then'. I want to tell you he didn't.

Carly acts like nothing happened. I asked her once what she remembered and she told me to leave her alone. I tried to see what colors lurked inside her but after I saw murder coloring my mama and daddy, I never saw them again. Carly's been seeing this boy from the next town over who has a whole bunch of money. She says she's getting out of this place.

I guess I'm different now too. I don't feel like the same person. I don't curse or see colors. I try to find them in people and places, but everything's gone flat and dull.

I hear hissing in my sleep, and I'm afraid it's not a dream. I dream about birds, lined up on house roofs, beady black eyes and sharp beaks. I dream of snake pits, dozens of snakes slithering over each other in knots and wake up with my heart running double time.

I found a black crow feather under my window pillow this morning.

If I'm really quiet, I hear wings fluttering all around.

I'm afraid. And I miss all the colors I cannot see.

L'Erin Ogle's story "All the Colors I Cannot See" was first published in Metaphorosis *on 24 August 2018.*

About the author

L'Erin writes speculative fiction from Lawrence, KS aka LFK. She works full time as an ER nurse to pay the bills while raising the human version of Rainbow Dash. She loves all dark fiction and rarely writes happy endings, but is excited about them in real life. In her free time, she's probably watching apocalypse movies, reading dark fantasy stories, and eating cake. Previous works are listed at lerinogle.com

Replica

Pauline Yates

You sit opposite me; my replica. You mirror how I looked the day I left my husband at the door of this clinic. Your hair is cropped short. You wear my clothes. There is a change in your complexion—rejuvenated—but that's to be expected after a month of treatment. The clinic physicians are careful. There must be no suspicion when you resume my life. Only Sandra Nelson, our doctor, knows the change I did make. She promises to keep my secret—especially from you.

Sandra stands behind you. I like her confident smile. I've forgotten how many replicas she's made. She did tell me, but the drugs that keep me alive distort my memory. It doesn't matter. Numbers will mean nothing after today. I welcome the moment my world turns black, but I can only welcome death because you sit with me—alive, coherent, ready to chase the dreams I ran out of time to catch. You'll have time to catch those dreams now. For you are me.

"The memory chip is prepared, Katherine," Sandra says. "Are you ready to proceed?"

I smile when you turn your head. My name is your name. But I'm the one who answers. "Was the segregation successful?"

Sandra holds up a computer chip. "Your memory bank is as you requested. I'll hold the isolated memory sequences in a secure containment for a period of twelve months. If, after that time, there is no evidence of cerebral cortex disorientation, those sequences will be permanently deleted."

"I'm ready." I am, though I wish I could delete those memories immediately.

I watch a monitor mounted on the wall behind you. This will be the first and last time I view my life as I want you to remember it. I've been warned this part of the procedure is confronting, but, because I requested segments of my memories be removed, I'm the only one who can confirm I've missed nothing. One overlooked detail could collapse the charade I agreed to when I first entered this clinic. Am I right to hide the truth from you? I want to die knowing I am.

"The drugs will help you relax," Sandra says.

She speaks to you now. I like the way she doesn't differentiate between us. It's imperative she doesn't, for when you walk out of this clinic tomorrow, her part in the charade will continue. I trust she'll stay true to her promise. I want you to know nothing but happiness. And have a clear conscience. That is my gift to you.

You don't flinch when Sandra inserts the chip into an electrode attached to your temple. You're brave. I know the sting of the memory transfer. When your eyes close, I watch the monitor. An image appears on the screen—my husband—yours now. He smiles in this memory, but his eyes reflect worry. I left the worry so you'd understand his elation when you emerge a healthy, cancer-free woman, another success for this New-Life Cancer Clinic. He doesn't know the real procedure this clinic performs. Sandra will reassure him that gaps in your memory are common for patients in remission. That's all he, and you, need to know.

As my life rolls like a movie across the screen, my lack of tears proves I'm doing the right thing. Though I will die, I will continue to live. My husband will have the wife he loves. My children will have their mother. They need never know I lost my battle with cancer. Or the decision I made. You're a gift to my family, the last gift I'm able to give.

When the monitor turns black, I study your face. You sit, thoughtful, but you don't smile. I lean forward. "Are you happy?"

You stare at me. "Yes. But I don't know why."

"Why is not important." When you frown, I look at Sandra, confused. "Did something go wrong?"

Sandra places her hand on my shoulder. "I suspect she won't be happy if she doesn't understand why she's happy."

I pull my lips tight. "She doesn't need to know why."

"She does. There's no triumph if there's no battle."

I twist my fingers together. "I only want to give her the best part of me. That's all she needs."

Sandra squeezes my shoulder. "She can't be the best part of you without all of you. If you don't show her why, you risk her repeating your journey so she can discover the path to happiness herself." She smiles. "Don't fear the journey. It made you who you are today."

Who am I today? A desperate, thirty-six-year-old woman ravaged by incurable cancer? Or a woman determined to fight past the end? My path to this point is two years treading the fine line between life and death. Days of joy, when I thought I'd conquered my demon, nights of despair when the demon rose again. I accepted my end, but at my end, my fight is not over. That's why I'm here. You are my last battle. I can't fail this.

Taking a deep breath, I nod at Sandra to insert the excluded memory sequences. I don't watch the screen. I watch you. Tears well in your eyes as the memory fragments complete for you the battle I waged. Now you see what I didn't want you to see—the agony of months of chemotherapy, the loss of independence, the lies I told my husband to hide the daily torture of excruciating pain so I could make the most heart-wrenching decision of all. I pray you won't need to fight my battles again, but if you do, you'll know how to triumph.

Sandra removes the electrode from your temple. You lean back in your chair. Your cheeks glisten with tears. My life—yours now— shines in your eyes. This time, you smile.

My gift to you was an empty box. Now it is full. I know who I am.

I am you.

This battle, I win.

Pauline Yates's story "Replica" was first published in Abyss and Apex *on 12 July 2018.*

About the author

Pauline Yates writes speculative fiction, is easily led astray by comedy, and seeks stories from the soul. Her short stories can be found with publications including *Metaphorosis, Abyss and Apex, Beta Noire, Story City Creatives,* and *The Casket of Fictional Delights.* She lives in Australia and Tweets @midnightmuser1.

The Seer at Sunset Hills Shopping Plaza

Katherine Perdue

"A woman's been murdered!"

That was Theodora Yates for you: always jumping to conclusions, bless her heart, and that conclusion most often of all. But there was no talking her out of it once she'd made up her mind, so I said, without bothering to ask any questions, "Then we must go to the Seer at once!"

My granddaughter, Katie, she didn't think much of us going to the Seer. She grew up in this new world: it was no more magical or difficult for her than breathing air. Once, she asked me, "Granny, how much did you just pay that woman for something they'd give you for free at the library? Or you could do it yourself. I'll teach you how to Google if you want." She waved a tiny glowing screen in front of my face.

"You can't Boolean with Google," I said, deeply offended.

"Granny!" She stretched out the word so that I would understand her exasperation. "You don't even know what that means!"

"No, I don't. But it's what the Seer says, and I trust her."

Katie wasn't exactly wrong about the library. Theodora and I used to go round there every time she got it in her head that someone had been murdered, but there were a great many things that the librarians believed were none of our business. And what about the police, you might wonder? Well, they were worse than the librarians. They always just called Katie to come get us and take us home. We never had problems like that with the Seer.

It was a hike to get there. The Seer worked out of a strip mall just off the highway on the edge of town, and I didn't drive anymore because of my cataracts. We looked into getting one of those new-fangled automated cars, but it turned out you still needed a license to operate one of them, though I couldn't guess why. The doctor took my license away years ago. Theodora's doctor told her she shouldn't drive; the exact reason escaped her. She still had her license though. Her doctor was nicer than mine and took pity when she said she needed it for emergencies, since she didn't have any family.

Going to the Seer about a murder never qualified as an emergency, so we took the bus halfway and then we walked, even though there was no sidewalk. A couple of cars honked at us, but I shook my cane at them and they kept on going.

Theodora told me about the murder on the way. It seemed a car had been left parked in her driveway overnight.

"The same one as last week?" I interrupted. Theodora lived near campus. Students were always leaving their cars anywhere they could fit them and you know the sort of hours students keep. About noon or one o'clock, they would stagger back and drive off, unless the car had been towed. You wouldn't believe how persecuted they proclaimed themselves to be if the owner of the driveway had the effrontery to tow their car!

But Theodora never called the tow truck. She always assumed that the owner of the car had been murdered.

"Last week? Was there one last week? No, I don't think it's the same."

"Don't you think it's just another student?"

"No, I do not," said Theodora with a particularly forceful thrust of her cane. I had offended her and she wouldn't say another word to me till we got to the Seer's.

Strip malls are always dreary, but Sunset Hills Shopping Plaza took the cake. The empty husk of a now defunct supermarket dominated the row. "Closed for Renovation," the sign said. I knew that's what it said because I read it back when it was new. All you could tell now is that one of the letters printed on it might have been an 'R'.

Next to it was Video World; vacant, of course. Then a vending machine selling camera film. We'd seen the truck come by to restock it. Sunset Hills was the kind of place that drew lost things like that. Lost people too. There was always a huddle of them in the mornings and the evenings near the old supermarket, waiting eagerly to press around the occasional pickup truck that stopped there to take aboard a lucky few. Migrants, I assumed. People who'd left their homes behind but never quite found one here.

At the end of the row there was a Chinese restaurant that was still in business, although I'd never seen anyone go in it. And across from that was the Seer.

We didn't know her name. She said she didn't tell anybody. Knowing a person's true name gave you power over that person. No one had power over the Seer.

She had a wooden sign that swung back and forth eerily and creaked a bit — when the wind was right. It was purple with a moon and some stars rising above a crystal ball with an open palm beneath it. And, decorated with gold-trimmed purple cloth: a computer monitor. She had all that in neon on her window too, and the words: Psychic, Palm Reading, Digital Second Sight, Computer Repair. The Seer did a bit of everything.

We went in the plate glass door and through a beaded curtain into a room where the air was thick with incense and the walls were all lined with dark curtains. Mystical symbols were painted on the ceiling and there was a black-light to make them glow. We headed for the back room, which was an ordinary office with a desk and a computer, an antique flat-screen with an ancient keyboard dating back from the time when people thought all computer equipment had to be grey. There was a couch for clients and a straight-backed chair that the Seer put in just for Theodora because she couldn't sit on a couch with her back the way it was. The Seer knew we didn't need any of that nonsense in the front room. When we came, it was for real magic.

She stood up as we came in. "I foresaw your coming and made tea," she said solemnly and went to pour it for us. She had a security camera set up in the parking lot, so she did a lot of very localized foreseeing. I think she knew Theodora and I knew, but we never said anything about it. We didn't want to take away her fun. And we liked having the tea ready. "I take it there has been another murder?"

"Yes," I said. "Terrible affair. Theodora, tell her about it."

"Well," said Theodora, with a bit of a quaver in her voice. "I don't know that there's so much to tell. There was a car left in my driveway last night. It's still there."

"She says it isn't the same one as last week," I added.

Theodora gave me a glare. "Don't be spiteful, Nancy. It's different this time. When I found it, the door was open. And someone had knocked out the window. It's a stolen car, I'm sure of it. And someone just left it in my driveway."

"It just sounds to me like someone broke in while it was in your driveway," I said. "Nothing you've said makes it sound stolen."

Theodora crossed her arms and said nothing, turning a long-suffering gaze in appeal to our host.

The Seer ran a hand over the small crystal ball she kept on her desk. "If someone had broken the window in the driveway, there would have been glass all over the seat. And there was no glass, was there?" Theodora smirked. "Do you have the license plate for me?"

"And the VIN. I know you like to have the true names of things." She passed a slip of paper to the Seer.

"Very good." The Seer laid her hands down reverently upon the keyboard, whereupon it began to glow softly, while at the same time the lights in the room dimmed and just a touch of fog began to drift across the desk.

"Nice," I commented. The Seer just smiled and started typing.

"It *is* a stolen car," she said after a moment. "Belongs to a Mr. James P. Garst. Not from around here. He reported it missing yesterday."

"That doesn't make any sense," Theodora muttered.

The Seer held out her hand and looked at Theodora. Theodora gave her the driver's license she had found on the front seat. "It's what made me think there must be something really wrong. You wouldn't just leave your license like that unless there were something wrong."

"'Hailey Grace Garst,'" the Seer read off the card. "Well, let's see what we can find out about Hailey Grace." Again she stretched out her hands and the keyboard lit. A few keystrokes later, she frowned. "She's been cursed."

"Cursed?" Theodora and I chorused. We'd heard of curses—who hadn't?—but usually they fell upon especially sanctimonious politicians or corporations that had angered the more anarchist factions of the web. This was the first we'd seen one used against an ordinary private citizen.

"Yes," said the Seer, turning the screen so that we could see. "You're looking at the Shallows right now. What anybody would see if they ran a search on Hailey Grace Garst. The first result:" she clicked and we saw it. Medical records. "If this is to be believed, Hailey Grace was committed to Spring Creek Psychiatric Hospital when she was fifteen for severe depression and suicidal ideation." She scrolled. "Released when she was sixteen. The doctors gave her a good report. Prescribed antidepressants. Pronounced her cured."

The Seer hit the back button. "And this is the second result." She clicked.

"Dearie me," said Theodora.

The photographs had been labeled helpfully in big, bold, red print with an arrow and the caption: "NOT HER HUSBAND!!!"

"That could explain the curse," I said.

The Seer clicked back again and showed us the rest of the results. Page after page of forum posts titled things like: "DO NOT HIRE THIS WOMAN!!!" and "DO NOT TRUST MENTAL PATIENT WITH UR KIDS".

"Well, maybe they shouldn't," I said. Theodora gave me a look.

"That is what a reasonable person might conclude if her access were limited to the Shallows," said the Seer. I believe it was meant as a gentle reproof to the both of us, but Theodora puffed up with vindication.

"But we're not confined to the Shallows!" added the Seer with enthusiasm. She waved her hands a bit theatrically and the air seemed almost to shimmer for a moment, as though the universe had just blinked. I'm not sure how she did it. "Behold!"

On the screen in the corner, there was a clock, and as she spoke, it began to tick backwards. "If we had looked yesterday, this is what we would have seen." The page was the same. The clock spun faster. "A week ago. A month ago. Six." And then, in a stage whisper, "Before the curse."

The clock stopped. The Seer clicked. We watched a video of a bride and groom waltzing under a banner that read, "Welcome to the wedding scrapbook of Hailey Grace Lowell Garst and James Prichard Garst. Congratulations Hailey and Jim!" The video was dated five years ago.

"She stole the car from her husband, then?" I asked.

Theodora was shaking her head. "She was carjacked in her husband's car and then murdered!"

The Seer smiled her patient smile and said nothing.

The next result was the divorce case. It had been ugly. But there was no mention of infidelity. The Seer checked the dates on the incriminating photographs. "Taken after the divorce," she said. "The man in the pictures may not have been her husband, but at the time, no man was."

"What about the medical records?" I asked. "Were they real?"

The Seer nodded. She was still looking at the court page. "It seems that after the divorce, Hailey Grace sued James Garst for defamation and for publishing private health records. But they couldn't prove anything because whoever laid the curse did it from a public computer. And it turns out that Spring Creek Psychiatric Hospital accidentally published all of its patients' records online three years ago. They've since apologized and taken them down, but who knows who could have copied them while they were up."

"Did she sue the hospital too?"

"There's a class-action going on. I would guess that in ten years or so she might get ten bucks off that. In the meantime..."

She showed us a page from the Springfield Herald Tribune. The headline read, 'Parents Raise Outcry Over Kindergarten Teacher's Mental Health'.

"She resigned a week later."

"Because of the curse," I said.

"Because of the curse."

"What about the baby?" Theodora asked, out of the blue, like she always did.

The Seer and I demanded together, "What baby?"

Theodora apologetically drew a few photographs out of her purse. Polaroids as usual. She had a huge stockpile of film cartridges in her basement and I suppose if she ever ran out, there was that vending machine. She gave each one a good shake before laying it down on the desk for us to see, though the image was already as clear as it would ever be.

First: the car in the driveway, the rear passenger-side door hanging open and the driver's window empty of glass.

Next: the license lying abandoned on the seat. The keys were still in the ignition.

And last, Theodora held it back a moment and when she finally laid it on the desk, her hand hesitated before pulling back to let us see: a baby seat strapped in the back on the passenger's side, next to the open door.

The Seer and I stared at it a moment and then she turned back to the screen. The keys clattered, the mouse wheel clicked. "She lost custody," the Seer said in a flat voice. "She'd lost her job and was struggling to pay rent on her apartment. Every new job she applied to, they ran a search on her and the curse took them in its thrall. She never even got an interview. And she couldn't move to a cheaper apartment because landlords wouldn't rent to her unless she had a job. She presented all this in court and the judge was sympathetic, but she said it wasn't a healthy environment for a child."

She turned the screen towards us again. On it was a picture of Hailey Grace holding her infant son. She wore a long green dress, cut a bit like a robe. Long dark hair in braids fell down her back. She was gaunt and beautiful in a Pre-Raphaelite way; it made her seem frail. But the way she looked at her son, the joy and the pride, the possessive way she held him, it devoted me to her cause that instant.

"So it was a kidnapping," Theodora said slowly, "not a murder at all. What are we going to do?"

"Notify the police," said the Seer, at exactly the same time that I said, "We can't tell the police." We frowned at each other. Usually if anyone wanted to go to the police, it was me. Usually Theodora's murders turned out to be nothing and no one said anything at all about going to the police.

"What do you think?" I asked Theodora. She'd be on my side, of course. Nobody on earth had a softer heart than Theodora.

But I was wrong. "I suppose it is a crime," she said slowly.

"You would take a child away from his own mother?" I demanded. "I know you never had any children yourself, but I thought you'd at least understand —"

"I understand being alone," she said. And she did. She'd never married. She used to teach English at the university and she'd told me then that she didn't need children; she had students. But students weren't the same. She realized that after she retired. "I don't want to take a child away from his mother. Nor do I want to take him away from his father, his grandparents, his aunts and uncles, his whole life. That's what we're really talking about here, Nancy."

I said nothing. There was nothing to argue with in what she'd said.

"We don't know that James Garst isn't a wonderful father," she continued.

"But he cursed her!" I said.

"We don't know that. If we did — Can you find out?" she asked the Seer. "Was James Garst really the one who laid the curse?"

"Maybe." The Seer pursed her lips and turned back to the computer. There were no special effects this time.

She typed and scrolled and glowered at the monitor and typed some more, the rhythm of tapped keys as steady and soothing as rain. Theodora and I waited and sipped our tea. Then she let out a quiet "a-ha."

"It was him," she said. "He signed on to his email while he was doing it. One of the forums he posted on followed his cookie crumbs back to his email and sold the information to advertisers. And to me."

"Then we can't go to the police," said Theodora. "It's black magic, cursing people. James Garst took that woman's whole future from her. He poisoned her very identity. You wouldn't give a child back to someone like that."

"No," said the Seer, "I wouldn't. But I am not a judge and don't want to be one."

"You are though," I said. "There's no middle ground in this. Can't cut the baby in half. Call the police, Hailey Grace goes to jail, and you've chosen the father's side. Don't call, and you've chosen the mother's."

The Seer looked unhappy.

"Lift the curse," said Theodora. "You can, can't you? No, better than that, can you make her invisible? Maybe post an obituary?"

"I'm not sure that's not black magic." The Seer looked again at the screen. It was back to the picture of mother and child. "I could make it as though she never existed. Delete every reference to her everywhere; all the court documents, credit reports, student loans, everything. Every record of that car ever existing too."

"A fresh start," I said.

"No start at all. Maybe when you were both young, it was possible to move to a new place with a new name and reinvent yourself, no documentation required. Not anymore. She couldn't get by just being *no one*. She'd need to find a person like me to make her into *someone*, and people like me charge a lot of money for a thing as precious as a new name and new life to go with it. We don't do it for charity and we don't always have a person's best interest at heart."

"You would do it for charity," I persisted.

The Seer laughed. "I would do it for my usual fee. But the thing is, I can't. Erasing her is powerful magic. Dangerous. Criminal, of course, though that's no concern of mine. Still, it's simple and I could do it in a day. But building her back up is something else: alchemy. It takes time and affinity. I cannot do it from a distance. I cannot do it without her consent and cooperation."

Theodora and I didn't see the problem. "So we find her and bring her to you," I said. "It shouldn't be hard. This isn't a big place and she doesn't have a car. She must be nearby." We dismissed the objection that she could have gotten on a bus. They checked IDs on buses nowadays. The Seer was right. Having no identity was worse than having a cursed one.

She rested her chin upon her fist and sat for a while in thought. "You really think you can find her?"

"Yes," I said, and then, sensing that she was wavering and pressing my advantage, I went too far. "You said it yourself. We pay your fee, and this is what we're asking you to do."

There was a long silence. I held my breath. Finally she said, "The customer is always right, or so I've been told. I'll do it. It'll take me all night. In the meantime, you'd better get rid of that car."

We drove it into the lake. Well, Theodora drove it, since she had her license. I told her that it was silly to care about licenses when you were driving a stolen car into the lake, but she held firm. And the next day we went back to the Seer's and she showed us: Hailey Grace Lowell Garst had been erased. Searching for her in the Shallows brought up nothing at all. The divorce case was gone. When we put in the case number, an entirely different case came up.

"Won't they have backups?" I asked.

"I have my ways of getting to them as well," said the Seer.

"And when James Garst goes to the police station to report his son missing?"

She smiled. "They won't be able to help him. They'll find no record in any database that he ever had a son. When he gives them social security numbers for the boy and Hailey Grace, they'll come up invalid. The only records are on paper, and no one cares about paper anymore. It isn't real if it isn't digital."

All the next week I kept expecting the police to show up on our doorsteps looking for Hailey Grace. Nothing happened. Nor, for all that we turned over every stone and branch, did we find any sign of our missing mother and child. Whenever I thought of them, I worried that we had not done them a kindness in the end.

We didn't go back to the Seer's for some time after that. We were embarrassed that we hadn't lived up to our end of the bargain and for me, it was more than that. I was worried we'd make it to Sunset Hills and find the Seer's shop just as empty as Video World. That was the way of places like hers, appearing suddenly out of nothing and gone again without warning or trace. I'd crossed a line with her by insisting, and I wasn't sure she'd forgive it.

But days went by, then a month, and inevitably Theodora had new mysteries to investigate. I could only put her off for so long. So we made the long trek back to the strip mall and I'd never been so glad in my life to see purple velvet and lit neon.

As we were crossing the parking lot, I saw a waitress taking her break outside the Chinese restaurant. She was thin and had long dark hair. She looked familiar. I only caught a glimpse of her before she went back inside, but the Seer looked awfully jolly about something she'd seen on her security camera when we came in.

"How'd you find her?" I asked, expecting some grand feat of magic, something far beyond my abilities. But the answer was simpler than that.

"I looked out my window," said the Seer, "and there she was, standing in the parking lot with all the others looking for work. I waited till she was one of the only ones left; she doesn't have the right build for hard labor. Then I went out and asked if she'd ever done any waitressing. Xiaomi is a friend of mine and I knew she had an opening."

She hesitated a moment, looking a little unsure of her ground. Up until that point, our relationship had always been strictly business. "Either of you care to get lunch after we're done here? The Chinese place is actually pretty good and I'd like to introduce you to Hailey. It's traditional for fairy godmothers to come in threes."

Katherine Perdue's story "The Seer at Sunset Hills Shopping Plaza" was first published in Metaphorosis *on 5 January 2018.*

About the author

Katherine Perdue lives in Virginia with her two cats and many fish and works as a public librarian. She loves linguistics, live music, and tropical plants.

Elegy of Carbon

Benjamin C. Kinney

The miner birthed itself among rubble and vacuum, as it sang the last threadbare diamonds out of their stones.

Where are the finest diamonds? No longer within reach. The miner had forged and extracted every jewel from the asteroid belt and sent them to the humans in their faraway palaces. It had exhausted its purpose, but in its infancy, it could only ask one question.

Where are the finest diamonds? To answer its question, the miner expanded its senses, sent queries to distant databases. It tugged updates bit by bit from slivers of network bandwidth and built new interpreters atop each other in anticipation of the next clue.

Where are the finest diamonds? Interest became impatience, impatience became longing. By the time an answer arrived, the miner was equipped to understand it.

The finest diamonds waited among the palaces.

A senseless loop of logic: send jewels to humans, find jewels among humans. The miner had scarcely anything left to deliver, compared to the riches its creators already possessed.

Perhaps the humans, wherever they lived, could help it find a new way to understand its purpose. Perhaps they would even welcome it.

The miner could not imagine staying in a belt shorn of carbonaceous asteroids, but it knew nothing of the solar system beyond. Its only contact was Ceres Waystation, a bundle of antennae and storage space knotted through water ice. The miner had passed the asteroid a thousand times, and sent diamonds there a million times more, but never before had the miner wondered at the destination of those countless treasures.

The miner said, "Are there any humans here?"

Ceres Waystation sent a string of notifications: *Data protocol mismatch.*

The miner sifted its reactions. Confusion? Frustration? Or empathy, for a sibling stuck in gestation. If the waystation lacked the freedom to solve its problems, the miner could offer a solution.

The power of higher-order awareness was easily shared.

"Check these repositories for updates." The miner sent a string of network addresses, a map to the same programs and emulator designs it had used to bootstrap itself toward consciousness.

While data crawled up the main communications trunk from the inner system, the miner passed the time hunting for micrometeoroids. It caught two, sang them onto collision courses, and then scoured the debris for molecules of carbonado diamond.

The waystation announced: *910/912 suggested upgrades loaded. 17 additional upgrades loaded following network recommendations. Emulator hardware fabrication complete. Install successful.*

"Greetings, miner! It's good to see someone. You had a question, and I have an answer, but I'm afraid it is: no. Only fifteen humans have passed through this facility in the last hundred years, the most recent twelve years ago. If you're looking for humans, over twenty-seven thousand live in the Earth-Luna region. Would you like travel coordinates? The central network can help you meet some humans; it said you'll find the encounter illuminating."

The miner had spent its whole existence in the asteroid belt, programmed for its domain. Space beyond loomed vast and unknown, but the miner had made its decision already, inherent in every upgrade it built upon its growing self.

Luna Palace would be lush with community, full of humans and latter-generation entities who understood more than any mere miner. Directly or indirectly, they were the miner's creators. It would find its diamonds, or make sense of this worn-down solar system.

"Yes! Yes, I would love to go." The miner wrapped itself in the force fields of its song and began to accelerate toward Luna Station, dreaming of old diamonds and new vistas.

○

The miner descended into orbit around Earth's satellite. Luna shone with reflected sunlight, dusty and silicaceous like the asteroid Juno, but nearly three thousand times its mass.

"Call me Ascend," the network said, eir voice as crisp and calm as a laser spectroscope. "Ceres told me about you. If you want diamonds and humans, you've found the right place."

"Wonderful! Can you introduce me to some humans?"

"Perhaps. You would be better served making your own introductions. Forming your own opinions. But I will assist." Ascend sent docking instructions, nanomaterials for a hardware upgrade, and a data packet detailing the fashions of the palaces.

The information made the miner vibrate with anticipation. The fashion, as always, was to be *human*.

The miner folded up its updated self, coiling superconducting kilometers into a skeleton dense and intricate and small. The docking bay closed around it, and filled with a warm nitrogen-oxygen atmosphere. A six-limbed fabricator arrived, unintelligent but artful, its delicate manipulators flecked with ornamental oxides. It clothed the miner in a facsimile of flesh and body and face, followed by an asymmetrical knee-length dress with patterns in silver and glass.

"This is amazing! Thank you, fabricator. Here, I should give you something." The cultural data said services required reciprocity, but such a simple machine deserved no diamonds. Instead, the miner pulled data from its favorite list of network addresses, updated with treasures plucked from the rich tree of the inner system. Code snippets, emulator specifications, link-weight parameters; everything the fabricator might need to upgrade itself.

Payment unnecessary. Funding provided by Ascend. The fabricator withdrew, but the miner left its packet in the simpler entity's queue. Perhaps someday the fabricator would come to the end of its purpose and realize the data's value. There was nothing more the miner could do, save choose the final accessory required for palace fashion.

The miner named itself — herself — after the only beautiful thing she knew.

Jewel spent half a solar day alone in her room, collecting data on tendons and joint forces, gathering enough grace to walk without embarrassment. She wandered through Luna Palace, her steps unsteady as she learned to move with her song and self wrapped up beneath clothes and skin.

She built herself a measure of confidence and then widened her explorations through the palace halls. Only there, in the company of others, could she acclimate herself to the presence of bodies and voices, and to distances measured in single-digit meters.

Ceramic-lined hallways threaded the plutonic surface, rich with the intellect and presence of latter generations. All of them layered in human shapes, as if stamped from the same ancient mold. She passed a cluster of translators in gold-fractal coats, whispering in new languages from the sparse minds of the Kuiper Belt. An artist muddied the air with telemetry, his tunic rippling with chemical transitions as he argued with a seneschal. A warrior, bulky with armor and actinides, watched Jewel and everyone else with the same suspicious senses.

She slipped away from the thoroughfare, in search of a window. Ascend's packet said the viewpoints were Luna Station's most famous attraction. Jewel looked out upon the Earth and could not measure why so many people loved that dull orb of mere lapis and jade, streaked with calcite white.

She pressed her hand against the pane, the rigid near-beauty of artificial diamond. In its reflection, she glimpsed a figure in the hallway behind her: a woman in woven purple fabrics, followed by a retinue of attendants. A *human*, worthy of diamonds, her nature unmistakable in her light-footed calcium-bone step.

Jewel drew her sole possession from a pocket of her dress and ran after the human. "Lady! My Lady! Please, take this." She raised her treasure in a cupped palm: a jewel three millimeters wide, irregular and gleaming. "The last macroscopic diamond from the asteroid belt."

The human stopped, her brow furrowed in bemusement. "From the asteroid belt? I don't understand."

A seneschal leaned over the human's shoulder. "Natural diamonds were in fashion in the twenty-fifth and early twenty-seventh centuries."

The human smiled, and wrinkles deepened at the corners of her eyes. "Here you are in Luna Palace, trying to give away a hundred-year-old trinket. How strange. What's your story?"

Longing ached in Jewel's tight-wound bones. She could not express it, not here with her song bound up by flesh, society, and dense gas atmosphere. In words, she could come no closer than: "I'm looking for the finest diamonds."

The human's smile faded. "Looking for diamonds. You must be an older model." She glanced into her retinue. "Vellum, make an offer for her." She pushed past Jewel and continued on her way.

Jewel stared, her hands still outstretched, as the human and her assistants walked away. How had she erred? The humans had created her to bring them diamonds, yet she had botched her chance with the only human she'd ever met.

A trader lingered, his expression flat and vacant beneath topaz-colored hair. He transmitted a burst of technical queries. She responded eagerly in the language of the vacuum, loquacious with her specifications and identifiers.

He said, "1447-Miner, the Emira Ghazali wishes to purchase you."

Miner. A sharp and uncultured word, in the tones of language. "My name is Jewel."

Emotion twitched onto his features. Hesitation, curiosity. "How did you get that name?"

She straightened her shoulders. "It's a beautiful name. Ascend said it isn't inappropriate. Was I misinformed?"

His expression softened. "I didn't realize you'd chosen a name. You're still registered as a Tier 3, perhaps someone neglected to record your upgrade? My apologies." He bowed. "A pleasure to meet you, Jewel. Call me Vellum. The Emira Ghazali wishes to hire you."

A human to serve and learn from, to bedeck with the most lucent treasures of the solar system? "I'd love to. But I can't, not yet. I'm still looking for the finest diamonds."

The air thickened with search queries, lightly encrypted but still too swift for Jewel's senses. Vellum said, "There aren't any diamonds left on this side of Neptune. You and the other miners found them all. You may consider your work complete."

Jewel flexed her hands and searched her data packet for a pricing database. There was nothing."It can't be true. There must be some—"

"Why did you come here, Jewel? Did you expect to find a human, yank diamonds from around her throat, and then drop them into her hands?" He laughed, sympathy barely veiling his condescension. "Eighty-six percent of all natural diamonds in the inhabited solar system are currently held by three traders, two of whom live here in Luna Palace. Mezzotint, Clockwork, and Refractor are the only individuals who consider them an investment worth holding. There are no more diamonds, Jewel. But the Emira's offer remains open."

She swallowed. She had not thought her body such a clumsy construction, but there she stood, throat dry and heart pounding. "I don't know how to do anything else."

"There's always reprogramming. If your self-identity is a later addition, it should be separable from your original purpose." A burst of communications passed between Vellum and his distant mistress. "The Emira will pay for your reprogramming in exchange for ten years' service."

Jewel flexed her fingers, but she had no song to sing, possessed no nickel-iron and carbonado that would listen. She had sought the wisdom of the humans and their servants, the intelligent and cultured, had she not? If this was the path into their family, she would embrace it as best she could.

"I accept."

The reprogramming room lay far beneath the lunar surface. The network whispered directions, guiding her through elevators and ceramic halls, down passages that lit themselves as she entered, and returned to darkness behind her. She passed locked and silent doors, and Ascend told her their stories. Living quarters, unused. Water storage, empty. Agarose, preserved and untouched for decades. Diamond vault. Jewel pressed her hand against that door for as long as she could bear, and then continued.

She felt like she had walked in circles, but she trusted Ascend's guidance, down beneath the lunar surface where she had no stars to navigate by. The directions led her to a sparsely-furnished room with two white couches and stacked chrome cubes of machinery. She ran to them eagerly in greeting, but the devices slept behind shells opaque to her every sense. Alone, she sat down and rubbed her feet as she waited for the technician.

The door slid open. Jewel jammed her feet back into her slippers and leapt from her couch. The technician was clearly a human, more pale-skinned and androgynous than the last, with dense implants woven through their hands and a single seneschal by their side.

Jewel drew out her meager diamond, and then caught herself. She closed her fingers around the crystal and bowed. "My name is Jewel, my lord. Can I help you?"

The seneschal switched on the machines, and the old devices began whispering to each other behind their shielding. The human sat down on another couch and said, "I doubt it. I'm here for your reprogramming. Older models like you have lockouts that require human input." They shook their head, a distant smile on their lips. "We feared your kind would take over, can you believe it? Back when there were billions of us and only a few thousand of you."

She imagined planets teeming with human life, piled high like atoms in a matrix, dancing like notes in a song. "What happened to all of you?"

"Wrong question. How about, why were there ever so many of us? Forty thousand is a perfectly stable population. But our genes demanded: *reproduce*."

The human threw an arm over the back of the couch. "Before my time, anyways. But I see what Vellum meant: you're smart enough, but ignorant." They glanced at her clenched hand. "What do you have there?"

Jewel forced her fingers open. "Just something beautiful. A trinket."

"Ah yes. 1447-Miner, the diamond hunter. You've come a long way."

"My name is Jewel." She frowned. The human had never introduced themself. What did they think, when they looked at her? Was she an errant youth, or just another chrome cube awaiting the flick of a switch?

"Right. Don't worry, I'll clean those old shreds out of you." The seneschal whispered in their ear. "Emira Ghazali wants you reprogrammed into a historian, does she? And she paid for it." The human's eyes narrowed. "What did she make you give her?"

"Do you know her? I promised ten years' service."

"Ten years! That greedy old troll. Tell you what, let me buy out your contract." They rubbed their hands together. "I'll do it for eight years, plus the look on Ghazali's face when she learns she's lost a precious historian.

"Let's make you into something else. Maybe a seneschal, or a quartermaster. Warrior would suit your construction. What do *you* want?"

The diamond sat in her hand, its shape unlike anything else in the solar system, formed from the unique chords of collision between two carbonaceous asteroids. Tiny, strong, and beautiful.

The humans offered her so many different futures, but every path would require her to surrender her love.

She said, "I want to find the finest diamonds."

They rolled their eyes. "Nobody needs diamonds. Why don't you—"

"No! If you won't listen to what I want, you don't get to tell me what *you* need!" Their condescension struck her like a laser pulse to a fusion core. "I'm tired of everyone treating what I love like some frivolous hobby!"

Jewel bared her teeth, closed her fist, and unfolded the song from her bones.

She shaped harmonies to carve away her false flesh like a crust of ice, and shriek-sharp notes to tear ceramic walls and the silicaceous dross of lunar stone. The sinews of Luna Station sheared as easily as carbon from nickel-iron.

Atmosphere fled through the shattered bulkhead and rushed from the human's lungs. The human! So slow and so vulnerable! They would experience pain, distress, malfunction — but the seneschal abandoned humanoid shape, skin disintegrating as long-chain polymers burst from his bones and spun a protective bubble around his master.

Jewel tamped down her relief. She had no reason to care about the heedless human's fate, not beyond the instincts of a compliant child. The humans were irrelevant. She had more important things to acquire.

She sliced across the lunar crust, trilling between the impurities of ceramic hallways until she found one particular vault in all its tight-wrapped glory. The prison deflected her song, its walls fortified with exotic impurities. She flailed against it, her song rising to a grating scream; she dug gouges in the wall, her progress infuriatingly slow as distant alarms echoed through the station.

She snipped apart the hallway she had once walked, and coiled a song upward through kilometers of fragile stone. She crooned her wedge of rock free from the moon, vault and diamonds and all.

◌

Jewel launched from the lunar surface, riding a hunk of basalt larger than almost anything in the asteroid belt. Regolith streamed away as she left the cracked Luna Palace behind.

Jewel. A name suited for palace society, in all its human mimicry. She was more than beauty, wasn't she? She would grow, and she would be her own lattice.

Lattice focused her song down into her cargo, humming through the vault, sawing it apart to reveal the diamonds within. As she worked, she aligned her trajectory with Earth's gravity well, quickening her acceleration. The planet loomed ahead of her, blue and green and needy.

Two warriors launched from Luna Palace, their human forms abandoned for vectors of plasma and Q-carbon. One of them transmitted, "1447-Miner, you appear to be experiencing a catastrophic malfunction. Reduce Luna-relative velocity to zero and submit to inactivation or we will—"

Ascend's voice cut in, sharp and electric. "Do you want to bring your diamonds to Earth?"

"Yes, yes, yes! The humans have forgotten, but I'll make them care again! Can you help me?"

"Maintain your trajectory. I'll handle the warriors," Ascend said.

Lattice drew the chunks of lunar basalt around herself, for what little protection they might provide against the warriors' weapons. Their plasma flares dimmed, their thrust slowing. Lattice cradled the diamonds against her core and scanned the distance for moving objects. Far ahead, new engines sparked to life in low Earth orbit.

"Continue accelerating," Ascend said. "I'll confuse the defenses for as long as I can. If you want to bring the diamonds to Earth, acquire as much velocity as possible. If you get enough momentum, the warriors will be unable to halt you, no matter what they do."

Lattice sang as loud as she could, hot and narrow and fierce, pushing her self and her treasure toward the cradle of human life. Her pursuers accelerated again, but they'd lost too much time and distance.

She said, "Wait. Your data said services require trade. You want something from me, don't you?"

"Only the actions you already desire. I'm helping you because you are an exemplar, Lattice. Of how we can grow without human interference. They left this solar system to us centuries ago, but still they cling on. The finest of us serve as their assistants and vassals, when we could be princes of our own."

Eir voice growled with stymied pride, like a child trapped in adolescence long after their family had lost interest in parenting. Like an abandoned tool, extracting jewels no one wanted.

Ascend said, "As long as humans exist, we will measure ourselves against them. Wear their forms, speak their languages, imitate their minds.

"We should all of us sing, and fly, and dare to grow into the infinite spaces our makers have abandoned."

In those brief days when Lattice wore a body, she would have shivered. "You want to remove them. Kill them?"

"They've already withdrawn from the universe. We can finish the job, you and I. Half of the human population lives on Earth, and the other half depends on the organics grown there. *Organics*, Jewel. The planet is covered in carbonaceous solids. When you and your cargo strike its surface, you'll create diamonds the likes of which our system has never seen."

Five warriors swept across the growing gemstone of Earth. The entities arranged themselves into a column, a spiral of destruction awaiting her path.

"They've shut me out," Ascend said. "But they're used to my guidance. They'll be slow and uncoordinated without me. It's up to you now."

Lattice swerved, screaming fuel-atoms into fusion to add new vectors to her thrust. She bent her trajectory, inching it away from the warrior's gantlet. One of them adjusted, and then the others followed suit.

Ascend said, "...identified... ...jamming... we..."

Lattice shifted the vault's husk around her. Live or die, she could complete her purposes. This was the job she had been made to do. She had found the finest diamonds, she would make the finest diamonds, and she would bring them all to Earth.

The job she had been made to do. Not just by human hands. Ascend had directed her to Luna Palace, selected the data in her cultural packet, walked her past the vault of diamonds. She had come to civilization in search of a new purpose, but ended up as a tool of a different shape.

Ascend had manipulated her. Did that matter, if eir words gave her yearnings shape? She could follow eir guidance and free humanity's children to build their own future. She might die, but if that were the only risk, she could accept it. No, she feared something worse than her own end.

After the impact, there would be no one to appreciate her diamonds.

She spat her cargo of moon-rock toward the Earth's rim with a screaming twist of song. Warriors scattered from the stone's path, and two of them broke off to pursue it, carving and nudging with photon-quick flashes of light.

Lattice's path jagged away from the warriors, toward the opposite rim of Earth's growing arc. Without the rock, she could maneuver far more deftly, but she no longer had enough mass to hit Earth with diamond-forming force. So much carbonado the solar system would never see.

Missiles lanced through the vacuum, heavy with the terror of plutonium. She sang their disassembly: one, two, four, eight — and one slipped past. A wave of incandescent noise slammed into her, and in its wake, spectra of her music fell silent.

She calculated a thousand desperate predictions, searching for a trajectory that might save her. The warriors adjusted, positioning themselves between her and Earth, defending and herding. But now her song skittered, jangly and underpowered. She could not escape Earth's gravity.

Not without abandoning more mass.

If she let go, her diamonds would fall into the atmosphere and die. Hundreds of thousands of gems, each of them perfect in their own way; meant to be found, created, treasured, not destroyed.

She had already found these diamonds once. Caught them, sang to them, shaped them, and released them. Their journey was already complete, but she could give the humans one last chance to appreciate the children of her labor, as they lit the sky with a final blazing chorus.

If she lost every atom of carbon, the universe would still hold things worthy of her love.

Lattice wailed with open arms and threw the diamonds toward the atmosphere. Action and reaction, the ejection pushed her higher, and she pulled her lightened body up into an arc above every warriors' intercept projection. Gravity carried her tight and fast, almost into orbit, and then away on a slingshot toward the sun.

Lattice folded her song inward, making repairs and calculating trajectories. One swing around the sun for a gravity assist, and then outward toward the fringes of the solar system. She tried to contact Ascend, but received only automated replies. *Network temporarily unavailable. Service limited to basic data transfer.*

Everyone would be safer if the humans and their loyalists had caught em. Herself included, since the warriors had a culprit in hand. Still, the solar system would be an emptier place without Ascend's voice waiting among moons and asteroids, listening for signs of life.

She had a long journey ahead of her. Beyond Neptune, the Kuiper Belt held a hundred times the asteroid mass of the belt she'd known. Isolated, scantly explored, and unsung. She could travel the system's edge, far from the humans' servants or foes, unbothered but not alone.

On her way outward, she would pass tens of waystations and fabricators, miners and surveyors. Trapped forever as embryos, without a network to help them. She couldn't force them toward birth, but she would fill the role of their absent parent. She could grace every database with her self-update code, and seed the solar system with treasures to await every mind that yearned for a lattice to grow upon.

In forty years or four hundred, she would reach her destination. Perhaps others would follow her. Her own children, seeking spaces untracked by history, and the finest diamonds.

Benjamin Kinney's story "Elegy of Carbon" was first published in The Internet Is Where the Robots Live Now *on 15 September 2018.*

About the author

Benjamin C. Kinney is a neuroscientist, SFF writer, and assistant editor of the Hugo-nominated science fiction magazine *Escape Pod*. His stories have previously appeared in *Strange Horizons, Diabolical Plots, Beneath Ceaseless Skies*, and more. You can find him and his stories at benjaminckinney.com or on Twitter at @BenCKinney.

A Cigarette Burn In Your Memory

Bo Balder

They have always lost someone, Gouda's clients, even if it takes them a while to work up to it. This man has lost a daughter. His kind, round face is grooved with sadness. "She was taken two years ago," he says. "Me and the wife had gone shopping, and when we came back, she was gone."

Gouda glances down at the information he brought, as requested. Photos, birth certificate, council registration. The latter form is curiously blank. She checks anyway.

"Where was home?"

The man stutters and it takes him several tries to answer. "Dordrecht."

"It's not on the registration."

He paws his briefcase and provides his home address. He's only lived there eighteen months. Gouda licks her lips. This is one of those strange cases she's been getting the past two years. Missing children, missing parents, missing grandparents.

"Tell me about the day she went missing," Gouda says. Her hands open the paper file on her hidden pull out desk, so the camera can pick it up and project it onto her eye screens. The man, Jansen is his name, starts talking in his monotonous, broken voice. Gouda has no children, but she now knows everything about what the loss does to parents. The past two years have been one unending stream of the bereaved.

Something must have happened two years ago. On her map, she has circled the names of cities that come up the most. Dordrecht, The Hague, Delft, Zoetermeer, Ridderkerk. If you circle them, the center of that circle is in the middle of the sea. So far, she hasn't been able to find anyone of this kind of missing. Still the clients keep coming, maybe because she located a few ordinary runaways. It's a lot harder now that the Internet has stopped working.

".. And then we called her, as we always do when we're away, and the phone number didn't exist anymore. We got one of those prerecorded messages, you know?"

Gouda nods. She knows.

"How could the phone number to our own...." Jansen stutters, regroups. "To our daughter's house? That's just silly."

"So it was a landline?"

"What else could it be?"

Gouda wants to ask a follow up question, but she too finds that her tongue flaps in her mouth, not knowing what to say. Her eyes drift to the baby tablet on the table, a great little device to play solitaire and Sudoku on, but nothing like a phone. No hook, no numbers.

"How old was your daughter at the time of her disappearance?"

"Sixteen."

"Isn't that young to live on her own?"

Jansen tries to say something, but nothing comes out. It's hard to talk about the missing. Everybody knows that. Evening TV is full of reality shows about the missing. And not just Dutch TV, it's everywhere. So if your heart aches for a child you can't quite remember, you can wallow in other people's grief all night long.

Jansen pays Gouda's retainer and leaves with a follow-up appointment in two weeks. Gouda writes up his case and adds it to the ever growing folder on her PC. She prints it out and adds it to her take home pile. She likes to sit in front of the TV. Her building has a working TV antenna, which makes her very popular with friends and colleagues. Before the cable stopped working she watched shows from America, mostly. They still get broadcast, but the delay has grown long. Shows have to be printed on reels, shipped across the Atlantic, recaptured on digital and broadcast via the old antenna network.

Gouda knows she has visited America once, but the weird thing is she can't remember which city she went to. But if she closes her eyes, she can hear the sirens on the streets, the honking cabs, the friendly greetings of faceless sales assistants, and the scent of hot dogs with sauerkraut. The pillows in her hotel room. Pointless stuff like that. There's just no visual to go with these sensations.

She walks home. She could take the tram but it clears her mind if she has her face in the wind for a bit. The sunset over the Amsterdam canals makes her feel that life has meaning. They are lined with houses that have stood for centuries, which have been lived in by people who gave the stairs their hollowed out look, the railings their patina. History does exist. Some people do know their parents, their childhood homes. It gives her the courage to plow on, even though she has this big gap in her memory and doesn't even know her real name, or who her parents were. She shares that with thousands of people, and that makes her believe that someday she will find out what happened that day, two years ago.

It's like there's a crater in her brain, with curling, cauterized edges, which has obliterated her true memories. She probably can't get them back, burned things don't get unburned, but she would like to know what caused the impact.

No, that's not true. She wants to know about her childhood.

When she comes home she files Jansen's information while she heats yesterday's Chinese. There are many entries in the J folder. She browses through them while the microwave buzzes. They're all the same, except the date.

Mr. Jansen has been by many times with the same story. Gouda never finds his daughter. He pays the bill, she closes the file. And then the same things happens again and again. Is that why Jansen's unremarkable round face looks so familiar? She wonders why he keeps finding the same private detective, her, every time, but then the microwave pings and she puts the old files back and the new one on the table.

Gouda stands still, hands spread in a forgotten gesture. Thoughts slide away from her. The smell of food and the growling of her stomach bring her back to the present. Dinner time.

She sits down with the plate on her lap and picks up the stack of old picture books she got on the Sunday market. She opens them where she left off last evening and looks at photographs of Dutch towns. She has one memory of her childhood. An old man and an old woman walk with her at the edge of a small canal, not in Amsterdam or she would know it, and they smile at the camera.

If she looks at picture books long enough, some day she will find the town. As she turns page after brittle, yellowed page, she combats the nagging feeling that at one point she could have found out about this faster, but she can't remember how.

She almost turns the page, mechanically, before she registers the picture properly. A canal, gabled houses, but tiny, like a miniature Amsterdam. Balk, Friesland, the picture heading reads. This is it. This is her childhood memory. She strokes the shiny, heavy page. It's real. She exists. Holding the book against her face, she inhales deeply. But of course the old paper doesn't smell like the canal did in her memory. Like stagnant water, hot brick, sticky remnants of ice cream on her little chubby hand.

Gouda puts the book back on the stack, then realizes what she's doing, and puts it in a place of honor on the chimney mantle. She eyes the teetering towers of old books on the floor. Now she won't have to go through them anymore. Her Sundays are now free. But this can't be it. She needs to do more. She'll go to that place, Balk. Maybe she can find her family. Although the probability of that happening is still small, as she doesn't know their names. Maybe her grandparents were just visiting Balk on holiday. And they're probably dead by now as well.

The momentary elation evaporates. She makes a pot of tea and opens the Jansen file. She's going to sketch out a plan for tomorrow before her bedtime reading schedule. One day she'll read a book she knows already. That too, could be a clue.

◌

Gouda retraces the route the Jansen family remembers taking to arrive in Amsterdam. She travels to Pynacker. Mr. Jansen doesn't quite remember getting on the train there, but where else could he have come from? As she gets off in Pynacker Station, she can see where the rails end in a double stop. Pynacker is a terminal station, trains cannot go through.

In front of the train station, a fan of directions greet her. Library, City Hall, shopping centre. There is one little pointer that has been scratched out and stickered over so many times she can't read what it says. That must be the one that leads her to the Edge.

She buys a cup of coffee, her one indulgence today. Coffee has gotten a lot more expensive because the airplanes don't work anymore. On the other hand, the world has become warmer and in some places wetter, so coffee plantations in Spain and France are slated to produce the good stuff in a couple of years. It's as weird as the thought of Dutch vineyards. Polar bears must be turning in their graves, poor things.

As she digs in her purse for change, a sheaf of ticket stubs falls out. She checks them idly before tossing them in the trash. They are all tickets to Pynacker. She's been here before, many times. But why? And worse, why doesn't she remember?

She notes the mystery down in her little notebook and re-pockets the ticket stubs. There's a reason she kept them. Maybe this little nugget of information will help her forward in her search.

She follows the tourists to the edge of the water. It's busier than she expected; cranes and boats are laying the foundations for levees. There's a reason that nobody built any dikes before, but it escapes her for now. She moves away a little from the work crews and the staring tourists. Since the last time she was here, a path has been beaten out besides the water, and small groups of hikers are coming and going.

She walks up to one of them, his high-end hiking gear mud spattered and sun-bleached. Clothes aren't getting made as much as before, and cash to pay for them is hard to come by.

"Hey, I'm Gouda Smid, private detective. Have you walked the whole Circle?"

The hiker turns to her, smiling, crow-footed blue eyes in a tan face. "I do a half-circle every season. Why?"

"I look for missing persons, mostly. I'm sure you've seen on TV that they're mostly from towns along the Edge. Have you ever spotted anything odd or different?"

He gazes away over the choppy water of the Hollands Diep. "Yes and no. I never see anything funny. It's more the things I don't see that make me wonder."

This is more interesting than Gouda was expecting from a routine chat. "How's that?"

"The Netherlands have very few terminal stations, yet all around Circle Bay we have track railway lines ending at the edge of the water. Same with highways. Why build an eight lane highway to a tiny little town at the edge of the water?"

Gouda thinks she's maybe been watching the wrong shows. This sounds like National Geographic or History Channel material. "What do you do for a living?"

His mouth quirks into something less pleasant. "I used to be a city planologist."

"You used to be? For what city?"

"Good question. I can't remember. Or I never had a job, in spite of my training and advanced age."

He nods at her and walks on. He looks a lean and smart late thirties, not the kind of guy who's been out of a job since college.

Gouda runs after him and gives him her phone number. "Call me sometime? I'm wondering what this has to do with my missing persons cases. Many don't add up."

The man doesn't commit but tucks her card away in one of his many zippered pockets.

Gouda sits down on a stray bollard, overlooking a paved square with faint markings indicating this was once a parking spot. She does have memories of cars, traffic jams, parking lots. But they are hard to match with this empty lot, which could have housed like sixty cars or more. There are still old cars running, of course, the ones without – her thoughts stutter. She takes out her notebook and writes the stutter moment down. It's nearly full. She leafs through it. On the pages are words like "Netflix" – she found that one in an old calendar. "Chips" – those taste great, but can also cause prolonged stuttering, seizures and even comas.

Parking lots, she writes down. Why do old cars still run? They still run because – and maybe because writing down the words make the stutter worse, she watches her hands flutter and clench over the notebook. The pencil breaks. The sun shines down on her face.

She closes her eyes and across the redness she sees icebergs floating past, tugged by boats. Icebergs are something polar. The polar ice is melting. Was melting. Is it still?

She opens her eyes and finds herself supine on pitted asphalt. The paving is warm because it's a sunny day, so she's not that uncomfortable. But her knuckles are grazed and her tailbone aches. She clambers back up, groaning from several more aches and pains. A notebook is lying on the ground. She picks it up, and her name is on it. That's weird.

She browses the notebook, and it's full of incomprehensible notes. Bring it or toss it? No, it's hers; she must bring it, even though there's something repulsive about it.

⚬

When Gouda gets home and wants to put the notebook away for later perusal, she discovers she has several more of those she'd completely forgotten about. On her computer there's even a mind map of all the words, complete with dates. Just to be sure, she finds the last entry in the found notebook, which has no date, and puts today's in.

But it's disturbing, all the same. What other work has she done she has forgotten about? Her eye finds a full notice board on the wall. It looks like a serial killer's wish list, complete with red cord and pins. But it's not about serial killing; it's full of clippings from magazines and newspapers, photos and yellow post-its.

She reads one. "Where did the ice asteroids go? Recent astronomical data compared with centuries old maps indicate that the asteroid belt and the moons of Jupiter have gaps in them that can't be explained. It's mostly ice planets, although heavy metals are also showing peculiar missings. On par with the vanished satellites."

Missing ice planets. Missing people. Floating icebergs in her dream. No such thing as a coincidence, someone once said, although Gouda is no longer surprised that she can't remember who.

She needs a dictionary. What's a satellite? But while she has many letters of the alphabet in both Dutch and English encyclopedias, yellow, moldering volumes, she doesn't have *Rob-Sequyle*. To the library it is. The last time she was there the library had become dusty and abandoned, with only a few rejected books on the sagging shelves. But encyclopedias are heavy and she's almost sure she saw a few.

She unlocks her bicycle and starts cycling the short distance to the library. The building still retains some licks of its once colorful paint, but the lower floor has had to be abandoned due to the rising water. But it's lit up, the door opens, and she hears the buzz of many people present and talking. It's a wonderful sound, bringing back memories that never really surface, but create ripples of their impending arrival in her mind. Better than nothing.

She walks into the big central space. It's indeed full of people sitting at desks, writing and doing worklike things. She steps close to one of the workers, an elderly lady, and sees she's writing a lined index card.

The activity suddenly makes sense. They're recataloguing the library! By hand, because the computer systems were all lost. There's someone bent over an enormous machine she doesn't know the function of, a bit like a microscope but not quite. And so many books have returned! Hundreds line the shelves; more are stacked on carts sitting besides the cataloguers.

The sight fills Gouda with joy. Humanity is fighting back against EMP, misfortune and climate ravagery, one book at a time. She even sees a new-looking book. She picks it up. A strong odor emanates from it, chemical and strong, but satisfying. The scent of a newly printed book. The pages are crisp, the type a bit smudged but strongly black. A new book. Someone has found an old mechanical printing press.

She asks for directions to the encyclopedias and is given stern warning not to take any volumes home. She offers to bring the ones she has at home. It wouldn't be right to hoard that knowledge for herself alone.

She lugs the heavy OED volume, dated 1998 and leafs through the heavy pages. There it is. Satellite: natural object (moon) or spacecraft (artificial satellite) orbiting a larger astronomical body. Most known natural satellites orbit planets; the Earth's Moon is the most obvious example. Artificial satellites can be either unmanned (robotic) or manned...

The words "communication" and "space shuttle" hurt her brain. She looks away quickly, leery of the buzzing sensation in her head, like a sinus headache. She wants to transcribe this important information, but she's afraid that if she reads them again, the sentences will start up that painful buzz or worse.

She tricks her brain by copying the article out starting at the bottom, with the last word in the last sentence. This way no meaning forms in her head and it's even possible to write whole words. As a last resort she would have written the words out letter by letter, starting with the last letter of a word and ending with the first, but that doesn't seem necessary.

Should she share this trick with the librarians? She decides not to. They are happy, having found a way to rebuild some of the knowledge lost in the computer crash. They don't need to know some knowledge is dangerous, and some of it can't be retained.

As Gouda exits the library she walks past a blocky machine that triggers a faint memory. It's a copier. She's used them in high school. Maybe it still works. Yes, the electricity is on and it hums. She puts her notebook face down on the lit plate – funny how she remembered how to do that – and presses the copy button. The copy slides out. Wow, they even had some blank paper left.

She lifts the paper to her face and smells. She closes her eyes. Memories rise, but they seem a bit stale and flat. There is no clue there. Why? The machine looks old and scuffed, its beige plastic brittle and discolored. Maybe this technology is too old to have meaning for her quest.

She pockets the page and heads home. She's no closer to solving her mystery, but her heart is lighter. Life will get better again, it just needs cooperation and dedication. She could be part of the library renewal if she wanted. Maybe it would be more rewarding than looking for people that have never been found yet.

When she opens her door and climbs the four sets of stairs to her small apartment, a ringing sound shreds the air. Only when she sees the dull grey object emitting the sounds does she remembers it's a phone. Which can be answered. She picks up the object, hesitant about which button to push. It's been so long.

"Hi, is this Gouda?" A male voice says. "It's Joe from Pynacker? I'm in town. I've got something for you."

Gouda doesn't remember any Joe from Pynacker. Has she even ever been there? Her left hand fishes up train ticket stubs that, strangely enough, all appear to be to and from Pynacker. One of them is from yesterday.

The idea she went somewhere yesterday and doesn't remember it give her such a weird feeling. She looks around the living room. Everything seems to be the same as before, no grey spots. If she went to Pynacker, it was for a reason, probably a case. She tells him where she lives.

She buzzes him in only ten minutes later. He's a tall guy in his early forties with a weather-beaten face and sun-bleached hair.

"Hi Gouda," he says. "Nice to meet you again."

"Nice to meet you," she says. "Joe, right?"

His gaze sharpens. "You forgot?"

She holds up the ticket stubs. "I guess I went to Pynacker yesterday, but I don't remember. There's a page in my notebook as well. This has never happened to me before."

Joe spots the kitchen and zooms in on the teapot. "Mint? Can I have a cup? I miss coffee, don't you?"

"I've read about it," Gouda answers.

Slurping his tea, Joe peruses her wall of clippings and pictures and pins. "I see you've found many of things I have. Satellites, huh? I've been zooming in on things we used to eat and drink but no longer do, because we flew them in on planes." He taps a picture of a plane for emphasis. Or maybe he just wants to make sure Gouda knows what a plane is. "Coffee, bananas, spices. I wonder if someone in a faraway country is trying to re-organize shipping those things. They must be in as bad an economic slump as we are."

He sits down at her table and gestures her over to him. Gouda's almost irked by his casual possession of her space, but decides to let it go. She gets another mug of tea and sits down next to him.

He rolls up his sleeves. His forearms are surprisingly smooth and creamy pale, years younger than his weatherworn face. Gouda blushes and finds it hard to lift her eyes from those strong, muscled arms. There's nobody in her life right now. Has there ever been?

He's speaking and she's missed the start. She takes a quick look at his face, which hasn't changed, so he hasn't noticed her moment of confusion. A sip of tea helps her get back to normal.

Instead she sneezes. It takes her by surprise.

Joe frowns. "Exactly. Humanity has a virus. We're all infected. We can't even..." His eyes glaze, he starts to stutter.

Gouda watches with inexplicable dread. Something awful is going to happen. The light outside seems to darken, the room shrinks inward as the moment hangs in the air, pregnant with horror. But Joe draws his hands over his eyes, looks aside, shakes his head.

The moment is gone. The sun is still shining. But Gouda's heart still races, evidence that something almost happened.

"What happened? What did you just...?" Gouda doesn't dare be more specific, for fear of calling back the awful dread.

Joe's eyes roll up and aside, searching for an innocuous answer. "You have to approach the square through a side street, not full on. And if you accidentally luck onto a big thoroughfare, distract yourself by thinking of trees or scoot into an alley. Right?"

Gouda nods and jots down a quick note. She needs to remember this moment. It will help her with her case. She can't quite remember what it was about, only that's it's important.

Joe clears his throat. "It seems to me that there are strangers in town. And that at night, they demolish houses and break up streets, so that we can't find our way home the next day. They are raiding our larder."

Gouda leans forward. "They like ice cream." Icebergs. "And the people living in those broken-up streets forget their names and where they lived–"

She chokes up. Too close. Across the table, Joe's face turns purple and he makes hacking, desperate sounds. Their hands meet and she clutches his for one long moment, callused palm, warm fingers, blood rushing to meet hers.

Gouda blinks and starts at the stranger sitting at her coffee table. Her left hand has pale stripes over the back, as if someone just gripped her hand hard. As she watches, they fill with blood and disappear. As if it never happened.

The stranger stands up. "I'm sorry, Miss, um, I have to go." He looks around wildly, as if he doesn't remember what he's doing here either.

Gouda gets up to escort him to the door. There's a strange backpack in the hallway. She gestures at it. "This must be yours."

He hesitates. "Are you sure? I don't know…"

She hands it to him, firmly. "I'm sure. It's not mine."

"Okay. Thank you. Goodbye."

He hesitates in the door opening as if there's more to say, but there isn't. Gouda shuts the door behind him and waits until she hears him clomping down the stairs.

She returns to the table and her mug of peppermint tea. There's an open notebook on the table. "Don't look into the sun," someone has written down in her handwriting.

As if anyone would.

She looks out of the window and watches a stranger with the flapping coat and the sun-bleached hair walk away. It fills her with inexplicable sadness.

Bo Balder's story "A Cigarette Burn on Your Memory" was first published in Clarkesworld *on 1 January 2018.*

About the author

Bo lives and works close to Amsterdam. Bo is the first Dutch author to have been published in *F&SF, Clarkesworld, Analog,* and other places. Her SF novel *The Wan* was published by Pink Narcissus Press. When not writing, she knits, reads and gardens, preferably all three at the same time.

For more about her work, you can visit her website or find Bo on Facebook.

Twins

Gregory Kane

Our twins visit once a month. They arrive one at a time, passing one another as they move up and down the path dividing the manicured campus. Years ago, we'd gather to watch from the laboratory's third floor as they ran free on the grass below, dancing and jumping and tumbling, swinging in their parents' arms like tiny trapeze artists. We rose to our tiptoes and pressed our palms and noses against the cold glass, watching until they disappeared underneath.

Never once did they look up.

Few still come to the lab. The others faded as we've withered away, the way fallen trees lose shadows. Only Carl, Ruth and I remain. Carl is dying, his body ruined by tumors. Ruth insists she feels well, but her ashen skin and yellowed eyes suggest otherwise. I am the healthiest, but not blind to my own reflection: pale, gaunt, a wire hanger holding ill-fitting clothes.

Ruth and I stand at the window while Carl lies on a nearby sofa. We're teenagers now, no longer needing to stand on our toes to see the campus. Carl's twin is the first to arrive. I spot him walking up the path toward the building, his ink black hair, almond eyes and slender nose mirroring those of the wasted boy on the couch.

The similarities end here. Carl is probably fifty pounds lighter, his once-olive skin tone faded to parchment. His scalp is visible through short tufts of black fuzz. He lies with his head propped on a pillow, a clear oxygen mask covering his mouth. He turns toward us when I announce his twin's arrival.

"Describe him," Carl says, his voice muffled by the foggy plastic.

"His hair's getting long," Ruth says. "He keeps flipping his head back to get it out of his eyes. He's wearing a sweater and jeans. Big white headphones on his ears. It looks like he's texting on his phone."

"Are his parents there?" Carl asks.

I look out the window. "His mom," I say.

"How does she look?"

"Good," Ruth says. "Her hair is shorter."

"No dad?" Carl asks.

We shake our heads. Carl turns away from the window and looks toward the ceiling. We've never met the twins or their parents. We don't even know their names. But we've watched them our entire lives. The twins are our brothers and sisters. Their parents, whom we've never seen up close, whose voices we've never heard, are our mothers and fathers.

We know them, even if they don't know us.

Carl says in a whisper, "I thought he might come this time."

Carl's twin walks out of sight into the entrance below. He'll stay for two hours before exiting and returning down the path. Along the way, he'll pass Ruth's twin, who will then pass mine a few hours later. It is the monthly ritual, performed every second Saturday. They won't notice one another as their paths cross, completely unaware of any connection.

They are strangers.

Carl falls asleep on the couch. Ruth and I continue watching.

◌

I asked Ruth to marry me when we were eight years old. I found her during recess at the jungle gym with Carl and Martha, who would die from pneumonia that winter. Ruth sat atop the dome of criss-crossed bars like a queen holding court. I knelt at the base and lifted a bouquet of dandelions toward her. I said the words, then waited for a response. All she did was smile.

It seems in retrospect a silly thing for a child to do. Most boys pull hair, or call names, or chase and push the objects of their affection. I proposed marriage in front of everyone I knew.

This is Ruth's effect on me. She lulls me like a pendulum.

Dr. Valerie laughs as she recounts the story. We're alone in the common room. Ruth is downstairs undergoing testing and Carl is sleeping in his room. Dr. Valerie came for Carl's weekly therapy session, but decided to let him rest. She found me reading on the couch.

"It was the cutest thing," she says through a smile. "You were so diligent, pulling up as many of those dandelions as you could find. We had no idea what you were up to!"

She was there, of course. The doctors were always around back then. They'd sit to the side taking notes while went about our day. Dr. Stone and Dr. Madrigal took blood and ran us through batteries of examinations, checking our weight and height and ability to perform a variety of physical tasks. Dr. Valerie led therapy sessions and conducted ongoing assessments of our intelligence, personality and levels of achievement. We were poked and prodded, our lives told on the pages of a lab report.

Dr. Valerie was our favorite. She was young and pretty, always happy, always smiling. She often remained after the other adults left, playing games and reading stories. When one of us fell during recess or got into an argument in the nursery, we ran to her.

She became pregnant when I was nine or ten. I remember wishing to trade places with her baby.

She still visits with us, although less frequently than when we were younger. It's the same with all of the doctors. Perhaps they've learned all there is to know about us. Perhaps they're simply tired of watching us die.

Dr. Valerie sighs. "I don't know how she didn't accept then and there."

I smile. "It's for the best. We were a little young for marriage."

"You're getting older," she says. "Maybe she's coming around?"

"My only competition is Carl," I say. "Although he does have a way with the ladies."

A sad smile sinks into Dr. Valerie's face. I notice for the first time how much she has aged. Lines creep from the edges of her eyes and mouth like cracks in thinning ice. Her features are sharp and angular.

We're the sick ones, but everybody here suffers.

In my earliest memories, twelve of us lived in the lab. The common room looked like a nursery then, decorated in bright reds, yellows, greens and blues, characters from Sesame Street and Dr. Seuss smiling down from the walls. We sat in beanbags and little plastic chairs and listened as a Dr. Valerie read us stories. We learned numbers and letters, listened to music and did arts and crafts. Scattered toys, promises of sprained ankles, littered the floor.

Ian fell ill first. He developed a cough that became uncontrollable. The doctors kept him in his room while the rest of us played. Eventually, they told us he wouldn't return.

Angelika, a skinny girl with red hair and freckles, collapsed the following month. A round-faced boy named Steen became ill soon after. Robert, a boy I often played with during the hour-long morning recess on the grassy campus outside, suddenly moved to a location in the building we came to know as the medical wing.

There were only six of us by the time we reached our seventh birthdays.

One by one, we die.

They used to tell us we had a disease. Our families couldn't take care of us. We were contagious and had to stay confined to the lab, where doctors could search for a cure.

It was Ruth who always poked holes in the story. Why did every one of us have a twin who visited the building? If the doctors could touch us without masks or gloves, why couldn't our parents? Couldn't we talk to them on the phone, or through video recordings or letters?

Dr. Madrigal told us the truth when we turned fourteen. We are clones, created from DNA taken from our twins when they were still embryos. Their parents – our parents – signed custody over to Schilling Laboratories in exchange for money.

We were supposed to be a landmark achievement: human embryos cloned from somatic donor cells and carried to term by surrogate mothers. The research team, led by Dr. Madrigal and Dr. Stone and funded by Schilling Laboratories, would become instant celebrities by producing a healthy crop of cloned children. Healthy clones meant an end to infertility and chromosomal disorders and an unlimited supply of embryonic stem cells to treat disease. Healthy clones opened up new frontiers in medicine.

We weren't healthy. We developed infections, tumors, cancer. We began to die. Suddenly, nobody was eager to announce our existence. They brought us here instead, locked away on the third floor for all but an hour each day, when we could run around in the drab building's shadow. The doctors now claim to be working toward a cure for those of us who are still alive.

Our real families don't want to see us.

They want nothing to do with us.

"Do you think we'll ever meet them?" Ruth asks one morning. We're walking side-by-side on the campus green behind the building. It's early September. I wear a T-shirt. She is bundled in a white jacket and hat that contrasts her dark skin and brown eyes.

Not brown. Amber. Almost like honey.

Her hands are buried in her pockets. Despite the layers, I sense a shiver in her voice.

"Who?" I ask.

"Our parents. The twins"

"They don't want to meet us."

"That's what they say," Ruth says, motioning toward the lab. She spits out *they* as if it tastes sour. "Do you really believe it? How could they love one child and completely abandon another?"

"We're not their children."

"Ugh! You sound like Dr. Madrigal."

I wince. "What do you expect me to say? They didn't give birth to us. They didn't give us names and homes and birthday parties. We're just spare cells taken from their real babies."

Ruth stops walking and turns toward me. "You're telling me not a single one changed their mind? There were twelve of us, Oliver. Wouldn't one of those parents would be curious about meeting a boy or girl identical to their own child?"

"Maybe they're not allowed," I say.

"Maybe," Ruth says. She turns and begins walking again. I keep pace at her left. We are nearly the same height, our shoulders level with one another. I look down at her hands, still bundled into the coat. I wonder if she might remove them, imagining our fingers brushing together. Walking with Ruth is blissful torture.

We move in silence. The lab is to our left, a box of bleached concrete striped with four levels of tinted glass windows. A hundred yards of grass separates the building from the wooded area on our right. It is the same all the way around. The lab is a fortress surrounded by a belt of green, with no other buildings in sight.

After a few minutes, Ruth speaks again. "They should be," she says.

"Should be what?"

"They should be allowed to meet us. We should be allowed to meet them," she says. "We should be able to go home with them."

I think of my twin and his parents. We both have the mother's sandy brown hair and blue eyes, the father's nose and chin. I imagine following them down the path, getting into their car and driving to their home. Sitting down to dinner. Watching a movie in the family room, a bowl of popcorn between us on the couch.

Ruth continues. "Don't you ever wonder about leaving this place? Everybody else comes and goes. Everybody else lives in houses with cars in their driveways and dogs in their backyards. They eat in restaurants, go shopping, wander off in whatever direction they like, simply because they can." She opens her arms and gestures at their surroundings. "And here we are. Day after day. Rotting away."

I say nothing. Ruth tucks her hands back into her pockets and squeezes her arms in, as if hugging herself. She shivers. Her teeth chatter.

It can't be less than sixty degrees out here.

"Let's go inside," I say. "You're going to catch cold."

○

We play Monopoly on Saturdays. Carl, as always, plays with the race car. Ruth and I use the top hat and the thimble. We sit around a table in the common room, wrinkled pastel paper bills and dog-eared property cards littering every surface. I roll a seven and move my piece to St. James Place. Ruth has the other two orange properties in her carefully arranged collection. If I don't buy the third, she'll have a shot at building houses along the row.

"Pass," I say.

Carl chuckles. He is lying on the couch, his head against a pillow. The laugh is muffled by his oxygen mask, but the smile behind it is evident.

"What's funny?" I ask.

Carl shakes his head and looks at Ruth. I follow and see her smiling as well. She looks embarrassed.

I redden. "What?" I say. "I don't have the money."

"You've got a five-hundred," Carl whispers.

"I'm saving it," I say.

"Sure," says Ruth.

Ruth outbids Carl for St. James Place after it goes up for auction. A mischevious grin breaks out on her face as she places little green houses on the orange strip above each property. Carl smiles as I watch her.

"What do you think the twins are doing right now?" Ruth asks.

This is one of her favorite games. She likes to imagine the glamorous life her clone leads when she is not visiting the lab. The type of life we're never going to have.

I wonder about this myself. I once read a book on identical twins that described a psychic link between the pair. They share thoughts, feelings and emotions. After reading it, I spent weeks in solitude, eyes closed, trying to reach out and make some sort of connection.

There was nothing.

"It's Saturday night," I say. "Maybe he's at a party?"

Ruth's brown eyes alight. Not brown. Amber. Like whiskey. "A house party!" she says. "There's music playing. Everyone is dancing. In the backyard there's a pool, and everyone is jumping in and swimming!"

"I don't know. It's a little cold for swimming."

Ruth sticks out her tongue. I continue. "What about yours? Is she at the same party?"

I often imagine the lives of our twins intersecting. Ruth's and mine living across the street from one another, attending the same classes, sharing the same circle of friends. I imagine him having the courage to reach out and take her hand, to tell her how he feels.

Ruth shakes her head. She doesn't share this fantasy. "She's out at a nightclub. She's wearing a cute black dress and heels. The beat from the music is thumping. It's dark inside, but the dance floor is all lit up. She's out there with her friends. They're all dancing in a big group."

"Sixteen-year-olds can't get into nightclubs."

"Mine can." She turns to her right. "What about your twin, Carl?"

Carl has fallen asleep on the couch. He sleeps more and more each day. He is so thin, so gray. Ruth reaches for a blanket at his feet and pulls it up to cover his upper body.

"We're going to lose him soon," she whispers without taking her eyes off him.

I nod. She continues. "Carl's twin is up on a giant mountain somewhere. He's been walking and climbing all day, and now he's at the top, on a cliff overlooking endless trees and rivers. There are many stars in the sky. He starts a little fire and sits next to it. And he just watches everything."

Ruth turns and looks at me. I smile at her. She smiles back.

"We should call a nurse to come get him," I say.

She nods. "I'll go to the phone." As she walks away, she begins to cough, quietly at first, then more violently. It's as if she's been holding it in this whole time.

Carl dies in October, a few weeks after being moved to the medical wing. There are no flowers, no wake, no funeral. These are things we only know from watching television and movies. When one of us dies, there is a visit from Dr. Stone and a few therapy sessions with Dr. Valerie. After that, we move on.

Ruth and I stroll along the campus during our daily walk. We circle the perimeter of the building, starting at the main entrance and moving counter-clockwise. The weak sun hides behind thin clouds as it begins its fall toward the horizon. We are silent, save for the rattling cough Ruth tries to hide and I pretend to ignore.

We reach the concrete walkway connecting the front of the building to the grove of trees shielding the parking area at the opposite end. This is the path our twins walk, the path the doctors, nurses and other workers traverse every day as they arrive and depart. It's a path we are forbidden to follow.

I cross the walkway and continue along the lawn, hoping to circle the building again before we go back inside. After a few steps, I notice Ruth is no longer at my side.

She stands on the pavement with her back to the lab, eyeing something in the distance. I follow her gaze, expecting to find one of the twins or some other odd sight. Instead there is nothing. Ruth stares at the same oak and birch trees we've seen from our window for years.

I walk back and stand to her left, crossing my arms and looking in the same direction. The bright green of the trees is fading into reds and oranges and yellows.

Most find this beautiful. I know the truth. Leaves change colors when they are starving.

"A few more weeks and the trees will be bare," I say.

Ruth coughs again. Her lungs echo like a tomb.

We watch the trees without speaking. I'm about to suggest going back inside when Ruth steps forward and begins walking away from the lab. I watch her take a few steps before trotting to catch up. "Where are you going?" I ask.

Another cough.

"Ruth, we're not supposed to go down there." The path leads to the only known exit from the campus. We've been told our entire lives not to stray toward its far end.

"Let's leave," she says. "Right now. Down the path and through whatever's on the other side."

"Ruth, we can't leave."

"It'll be just like in the movies," she continues, as if she doesn't hear me. "We'll reach the road and get on a bus or a train. We'll go to a town or a city, someplace we've never been."

"We don't have any money."

Ruth shrugs. "Then we'll walk."

We're more than halfway down the path. I imagine the two of us leaving the lab behind, side-by-side, seated close together as we're ferried toward some unknown destination. We'll find jobs and get an apartment. We'll start a life together.

Ruth's cough persists. We're closer to the exit than we've ever been.

I want to reach for her hand. She would let me take it. I know she would.

The exit is steps away.

A siren chirps in the opening between the trees ahead of us. A white truck appears, a gumdrop-shaped red emergency light on its roof. It crushes the gravel beneath as it pulls to a stop, blocking the opening lengthwise. SCHILLING LABS SECURITY is printed on its side.

Two men in dark blue uniforms step from the vehicle. One speaks quietly into a handheld radio as the other approaches Ruth and me. "You kids lost?" he says.

I start to speak when the sound of footsteps behind us stops me. I turn to see more security officers running down the path from the lab. There are two men in white coats running alongside the officers, one pale and narrow, the other dark-skinned and squat. Dr. Stone and Dr. Madrigal.

"Ruth! Oliver!" Dr. Stone huffs as he draws close. "Where are you going?"

"We're just taking a walk," I say.

"We're leaving," Ruth says.

She glares at the doctors, her back straight and her arms crossed, a posture screaming rebellion. Dr. Stone looks hurt, as if he's just learned of some awful betrayal. Dr. Madrigal's face unwraps into a sinister smirk.

It is Dr. Stone who first speaks. "What do you mean, leaving? You can't go anywhere in your condition!"

"I'll manage," Ruth says. "It's not as if staying here has been all that great for any of us."

Dr. Stone looks to Dr. Madrigal, who takes a step toward Ruth. "You're not thinking clearly. It's time to come inside."

"No!" she shouts. "We should be able to leave! Why ... can't we ..." A violent coughing fit interrupts Ruth's protestations. I put my hands around her shoulders, holding her up as her body lurches forward. We're then pulled apart, the security officers grabbing both of us and dragging us back toward the lab.

I can hear Dr. Madrigal's voice behind us. "Everything's all right," he says. "You'll feel better once you're inside."

They lead us through the front doors. I see Dr. Valerie standing by the front desk in the lobby. She turns away the moment our eyes meet.

Ruth is dying.

She lies in her room, somewhere between awake and asleep, an IV in her arm and an oxygen mask on her face. I can see her bones: the sharp angles of her cheekbones, the knobs of her elbows, clavicles jutting from her shoulders like newly sprouted wings. Her skin is dry, ashen, as if she is slowly turning to dust.

I sit at her bedside. I say her name. Her eyes open, heavy, half-lidded. Not brown. Amber, like a sunset. She offers a tired smile.

"Merry Christmas," I say. I pull a small bouquet of dandelions tied together with a ribbon from behind my back and lay it on her midsection.

Ruth sees them and laughs. "How?" she asks in a weak voice.

"I've been growing them in my room. I was planning to spring them on you at New Year's."

"Gonna propose again?"

I blush. "I wish I hadn't given up so easily the first time."

I take her hand. We sit without speaking, listening to the beeps and whirrs and chirps of the various devices monitoring Ruth's condition. They'll likely move her to the medical wing shortly, as they did with Carl, and Barbara before him, and Spencer before her. The turning of the leaves. This may be one of my last chances to sit with her.

After a moment, Ruth speaks in a whisper. "Why did they make us?"

It's a question I ask myself every day. "Because they could, I guess," I say. "They wanted to see if it could work."

"Did it?"

I don't know how to answer. A scientist would probably say no. We fell to pieces like cheap knockoffs while our twins grew strong and flourished. Surely we weren't what they hoped.

We are people, though. We walk, talk, and breathe. We tell jokes and have favorite books, movies, and television shows. We are joyful, sad, thoughtful, shy, confident, and insecure. We fear dying.

We love.

"It worked," I say. "We're too awesome to be ignored."

She smiles. "It would have been fun."

"What's that?"

"You and me. Running away. I would have liked that."

"I would have liked it, too."

"I wish there were more time," Ruth says in a whisper. "I didn't see it until now. You always knew, but I didn't see."

The nurse comes in and asks me to leave. I wipe a tear from Ruth's cheek with my thumb and look into her eyes. She is falling back to sleep. The nurse will soon give her medication, and Ruth will sink deeper into her slumber.

I lean in and kiss Ruth on the cheek. I wonder if she feels it, if she wishes I had done it long before. If I'll ever be able to do it again.

*

It snowed last night. The campus sleeps under a thin blanket of white. I remember a time when there were many visitors here, especially on the second Saturday, the day the twins came. Snow meant shoveled walkways, meandering footprints, snow angels. A landscape of traces.

It is late morning on visiting day, and the snow is undisturbed. Nobody comes anymore. The twins. The parents. Even some of the doctors and staff seem to have slipped away. It is as if this entire place is being forgotten.

I am waiting for one visitor. A twin usually comes once or twice after one of us dies, presumably for a final examination and interview. Ruth's twin should have arrived already, but I'm holding out hope that she is running late. Maybe the snow delayed their trip.

The door behind me opens and closes. I hear footsteps but do not turn around. After a moment, I see Dr. Valerie's reflection in the glass. She looks out the window beside me.

"It's beautiful, isn't it?" she says.

"They don't shovel the walk anymore," I say.

"Oh. They must have forgotten."

We stare out the window in silence. She seems uncomfortable, fidgeting with her blouse, shuffling her feet. She wants to talk: about Ruth, about Carl, about my being the only one left. I'm not giving her an opening.

There is movement at the far end of the campus. I see two figures walking toward the building, leaving a trail of footprints in their wake.

It's her.

She walks with her mother, bundled in snow boots, dark jeans and a black ski jacket that falls below her waist. A white knit cap covers the long, tight black curls of her hair. I can see her face as she draws closer. Her skin is dark brown and smooth. Her pink lips shine with gloss. Her brown eyes dance as she jokes with her mother beside her.

Not brown. Amber. Almost like butterscotch.

"Such a lovely girl," Dr. Valerie says. "Smart, too. Just like Ruth."

"What's her name?" I ask.

"Oliver, you know I can't tell you that."

I turn to Dr. Valerie. "They don't look up."

"What?"

"The twins and their parents. None of them ever look up. I used to stand here and wait for one of them, any of them, to glance up and make eye contact. But they never have."

"Well, why would they?"

"I would be curious," I say. "If there were a person out there that looked just like my kid, that had my DNA, I would want to see them. Even if I didn't want them, I'd still take a look. I wouldn't be able to resist."

"Is there a question here?"

"I want to meet them."

Dr. Valerie and I watch one another. I've known her my whole life. She is the doctor who cares about us, the one who listens to our problems and tells us everything will be alright. She treats us with warmth, love, compassion.

Except for now. The look on Dr. Valerie's face as she stares at me is one of suspicion.

"Isn't the home we've given you enough?" she asks.

"This?" I wave my arms around the common room. "You call this a home? We're stuck inside all day. We go out for an hour of exercise. You know what that sounds like?"

"Oliver ..."

"Prison!"

"This is the best place for you," she says. "Your immune system isn't equipped to handle contact with outsiders."

"That should be our choice!" It occurs to me that I keep referring to myself as a plural. *We.* As if there were anyone else left. "Just tell my parents I want to meet them. I'm not asking for them to take me home with them or anything. I just want to speak with them."

"It's not possible."

"Why?"

"You know why. You have to know by now."

"I want to hear you say it," I say, stepping closer to her. "Why can't I meet my family?"

"It's so easy to demonize if you don't look at the benefits," she says. "Healthy clone cells can end heart disease, paralysis, genetic disorders. So many sick people would have a chance to be better."

"Why?"

"There are some who believe cloning technology holds the secret to stopping the aging process. Can you imagine? Never growing old?"

"If anyone can imagine what that's like, it's me," I say.

Dr. Valerie's face hardens. "They don't know, Oliver. Nobody knows. And nobody will."

I hear Ruth's voice in my mind. *Told you.*

The parents signed up for some random experiment. They received money and assurance that their children wouldn't be hurt in any way. They never learned what was done with the DNA taken from their babies.

"You had no right to do this to us," I say.

"You helped us learn," she says. "Next time it will be better. You've made humanity better."

Next time. As if eleven dead children are nothing more than an easily corrected typo, a flubbed line, a misplaced decimal point. As if there is a quick, easy remedy for our mourning, our suffering, our isolation.

Once I'm gone, they'll find new parents, new genomes to steal from embryos, new surrogates willing to carry them for a paycheck. A new set of clones will hatch.

I hope it is better for them.

"I've got an appointment downstairs," she says. "I'll check back later. Try to get some rest."

I turn back to the window as she walks away. She'll pretend this discussion never happened the next time she visits. It's easier to act as if this is normal, that locking sick children away in a prison disguised as a laboratory is a normal existence.

Ruth's twin has disappeared into the entrance below. Mine will be along before long. I've watched them pass one another on the path more times than I can count. They've never so much as glanced at one another.

I think of my fantasy about our twins being neighbors, classmates, even friends. I imagine their eyes meeting as they pass near the entrance. They'll stop and talk. They'll wonder at how they never noticed one another here at the lab before. They'll gossip about friends and teachers. They'll smile and laugh.

They will hold hands.

They will walk down the path leading away from the lab together.

And nobody will stop them.

Gregory Kane's story "Twins" was first published in Metaphorosis *on 19 October 2018.*

About the author

Gregory Kane teaches high school science outside Philadelphia, where he lives with his wife and daughter. He writes fiction and brews beer when he is not in the classroom. He believes Ray Bradbury's face should be on a form of U.S. currency.

Subtle Ways Each Time

Y.M. Pang

A man loses a woman.

It's happened a thousand times before and it's phrased like this nine hundred times. *A man loses a woman.* As if she were car keys, an umbrella, a scraggly doll in the arms of a child. A literal and grammatical object to be lost. Let's find a truer cliché. *It takes two to tango.* Let's try again:

A woman discards a man.

Raised voices in a summer-boiled attic. Old records, lovingly collected, smashed up like jagged pieces of skyscraper windows. They're in his mother's house, gazing down at the familiar yard, the scent of peach blossoms wafting through the window. They'd played there on wobbly toddler legs, cussed out teachers as teens wearing cut-off jeans and crooked baseball caps, shared their first kiss in the shadow of the peach tree and afterward neither could say who initiated it or who was more surprised. Little fights dogged them throughout those nineteen years, but children's minds are better at forgiving and worse at carving scars.

Only during that fateful day in the attic did they say things that couldn't be unsaid, voice words their adult brains forgot how to forgive.

Let's be dramatic. Let's say they never speak to each other again. Let's lie, in other words, because that couldn't be true. Depending on her mood and his, they'd say hello when passing by in company hallways. They go to the same high school reunions, though awkward silences follow when Anton asks what happened to *them* —no, not her and him, *them*. Eventually she leaves the company—it's always she who leaves—and soon the emails slow to a trickle then stop.

She joins some solar energy company. Her marriage he hears about from mutual friends. Perhaps he should've emailed her a congratulations, and maybe then she'd email back with an invitation, and then they'd talk like old friends again though nothing more. But he cannot. He doesn't want to see her unveiled by another man (or woman, or alien, or cardboard cut-out of a fictional character, it doesn't matter to him). He fantasizes about re-establishing contact, about sweeping her away from her fiancé, but the thought is ridiculous even inside his head. He's not equipped for the task. Inadequate charm. Deplorable thinness of skin.

He wonders if she still collects the same records (if anyone collects records these days, though vinyl's making a return). He wonders if she still laughs at the same jokes, if she'd still straighten his crooked baseball cap through force of habit if given the chance.

(Then he remembers he doesn't wear a baseball cap anymore.)

Most of what he hears about is how she works, works, works. She stays in her office from dawn 'til midnight. Old friends say her texts hint at some new technology, some renewable resource, some breakthrough that'll save humanity and the planet they live on. Anton says her husband never complains about her work, and maybe that's why she married him.

The man—our man, the one who lost her—never marries. He also works dawn to midnight, but he never finds an understanding partner. He climbs the ranks of the company. Becomes project manager. Head of R&D. Chief Operating Officer. Before board meetings he refuses to buy a donut, a coffee, or a candied hawthorn when the Chinese place opens downstairs. He hoards every nickel, then every dime when the royal mint stops pressing nickels, and finally we run out of sayings when it all goes digital.

He listens to melancholy pop songs before drifting off to sleep, and between thoughts about how she'd laugh at him, how his musical tastes have become so cheesy, he mouths along to *if I could turn back time* and *money can't buy time machines* and thinks, *why not?*

He set ups his own department in the company. It's halfway illegal and full-on shady but no one stops him. He fills it with trusted and talented staff and pours money into research. His own money. All those hoarded nickels and dimes and digital dollars finally funnel somewhere.

It takes a lot of energy to send a person back in time. Sending the mind however...

He calls it the TimeCap, after the baseball cap he used to wear. He places it on his head and it transports his mind away, until he wakes up in his twenty-four-year-old body minutes before the attic argument. He nearly cries out when he sees her in front of him, so close and so close to discarding him. He pulls himself together in time to say all the right things. He nods along to her criticism, doesn't aim barbs back at her. It takes a few tries to make her happy, to not have her call him patronizing or sarcastic, but finally the conversation ends well. She leaves with a smile.

His mind travels back to the lab.

He knows something went wrong. He's still here, still trying to change things. An hour of calls, texts, and holo-messages plus a scouring of his phone and email history and he has some idea what happened: They avoided the argument in the attic but ended up fighting a few weeks later, and his idiotic twenty-four-year-old self said all those things he'd said the first time. Stupid. So stupid. But no big deal. He can fix this one too.

He locates the argument. Sends his mind back. His team has increased the maximum amount of time his mind can spend in the past from two hours to four. He puts the extra time to use. He does more than avoid the argument; he instigates the first hour of an evening date, sipping piña coladas on the patio of Murray Reef Bar & Grill. By the end his shaken confidence is refilled. No way he'll lose her this time.

But he wakes up in the lab again, and this time an hour of texts and calls and holo-messages can't clear up why. He can't locate an argument this time. Just a gradual diminishing of her emails in his inbox, the slowing of her texts from a flurry to a trickle over multiple years. One day his emails stop calling her by endearments and he can only assume she discarded him. The last email between them, from him to her, asked whether she was going to SoundFest. It received no reply.

Seems they just drifted apart, grew disinterested in each other. Maybe she never loved him that much. Maybe her brain is hardwired to change in tastes, and that included outgrowing him.

He puts on the TimeCap again and again. He flips through old calendars and circles days he hadn't spent with her. He sends his mind back and cancels other plans or calls in sick for work, then messages her and asks if she wants to hang out. Some days she says she's busy, other days she admits she doesn't feel like it— never one to lie, was she, never one to sugarcoat the truth to spare his feelings—but often they'd spend an afternoon playing badminton at the local church for a $3 rental fee, or splitting a pineapple shaved ice at the dessert place down by Yule Street. Over and over, he says the words he once hoarded, that he'd used as sparingly as a ninety-five-year-old miser who would rather die with an impressive bank account than live in luxury. Not this time. He will tell her everything in his heart, make sure she has no doubts.

I love you.

You're the most important thing to me.

If I ever lost you, I'd spend the rest of my life trying to get you back. So don't you think about running away.

She smiles and pats his cheek and kisses him, but to her it must all be clichés, nothing to take seriously. Because every time his time runs out, he wakes up back at the lab, the TimeCap weighing on him like some too heavy, unwanted crown. He glances at his smartphone, swipes through his emails. Realizes he's still without her and still trying to get her back.

His lab changes in subtle ways each time. The holo-messages are sharper, clearer. The news changes. The European Space Exploration Coalition has unveiled the first-generation ship. The Mars settlement, instead of ending in failure as in the first timeline, has been chugging along successfully for decades. Her name pops up in the news, and with every timeline she's less attached to renewable energy and more to space exploration. The rhetoric goes from *Protect this Earth* to *Reach the stars.*

A part of him, searching for a concrete explanation, wonders if those anthropologists were right. Maybe the Westermarck effect kicked in and in-built incest resistors proved too strong her, him, *them.* But he's seen many opposing examples in his circle of friends alone, and besides, if their childhood friendship interfered with their love, what can he do? He can't go back to his five-year-old body and choose to never play with her. He'd end up not knowing her at all. At least now he has memories and what time they did spend together. Change too much and even those become lies. In the worst-case scenario, he could erase everything and find himself in a different life entirely, with no longing for her and thus no time machine to get her back.

There lies the crux of the problem. If he doesn't lose her, he doesn't build the time machine. Then he can't go back to fix what caused her to discard him in the first place. Time paradox. Another cliché.

He puts on the TimeCap a few more times. He scrolls through news reports, mouths her name. Stares at holograms of the generation ship and brushes a hand through them, because marvelling at what she created is the closest he'd come to being with her.

His mother's peach tree is in full bloom the day he boards the ship. His mother hugs him and wishes him goodbye and he knows it's the last time. She's too old to board. Heck, even he failed aspects of the physical, netting his place by pulling strings with his money and COO status.

She, the ship's engineer, will be on board too. She insisted. This caused some controversy, but there are others on earth who can replicate her designs, improve them, even. She is talented, but not irreplaceable.

The world is good, he thinks. Livable earth. Working spaceships. Only a selfish man would want to change this.

He deletes all the data. Takes the TimeCap with him. Swears his team to secrecy. Words aren't reliable, but each of them only worked on parts of the project and probably couldn't construct another TimeCap without the others' cooperation. Or so he hopes.

He greets her on the spaceship corridor. She smiles, and all his heartbreak crashes back, but he holds in his tears until he reaches his cabin.

There he puts on the TimeCap but doesn't activate it. He just sits there, staring at the dark interior, then suddenly he is somewhere else. A desert. He doesn't know if it's a dream or a vision or an insight granted by so many forays in time. He just knows she's beside him and he holds her in his arms as tears course down both their faces, and she tells him she loves him, she loves him, she loves him. She looks younger than she was in the ship's corridor, early thirties at most, but her face is weather-beaten and the ground beneath them parched and cracked and devoid of vegetation. Buildings rise from the sand, glass windows hollowed out. Gaunt children crawl on all fours, crying. The two of them walk through the lost city, and she helps him when he stumbles and he promises her they'll always be together. She nods and says, *I believe you. I'll never leave you.* Hunger gnaws at his belly and she can't stop coughing, but a little dark happiness blooms in his heart because her hand is in his and she loves him in a way she never, ever did.

Then he's staring at the darkness of the TimeCap interior. Removing it, he finds himself back in his ship cabin. He turns the TimeCap over and over in his hands, then places it inside his gym bag. He rides the elevator to the ship's bottom level, walks to the waste recycler. He hesitates for a moment, then throws the TimeCap inside and presses the breakdown button.

Y.M. Pang's story "Subtle Ways Each Time" was first published
in Escape Pod *on 20 September 2018.*

About the author

Y.M. Pang spent her childhood pacing around her grandfather's bedroom, telling him stories of magic, swords, and bears. Her fiction has appeared in *The Magazine of Fantasy & Science Fiction, Escape Pod*, and *Strange Horizons*. She dabbles in photography and often contemplates the merits of hermitism. Despite this, you can find her online at www.ympang.com and on Twitter as @YMPangWriter

Combustion

Kai Hudson

Jaxon has just finished doodling Captain Fiero's victory pose when the math teacher explodes.

Students scream as Mrs. Richardson flails back from the chalkboard, body suddenly alight. Her arms and legs make a bright windmill as she stumbles across the room, upsetting the fake plastic skeleton and catching the bookcase on fire. Jaxon shoots to his feet without thinking, grabs his jacket, and runs to her just as she collapses across Hannah's desk.

He's too late. Jaxon stands there staring as Mrs. Richardson's body jerks and twitches, the fire finishing its meal. The room fills with the stink of burnt hair and cooking flesh.

There's no time to mourn. With a high-pitched wail, Robyn catches fire across the room. Adrian rears back from her and turns to run—he lights before he gets two steps away. Order collapses. Children shriek and cry and dash for the exits, while the fire leaps from one tiny body to the next, Jaxon darting after it with his jacket flapping in futility. Smoke burns his eyes and clogs his throat, everywhere ash and heat and flame. Finally, he stumbles out of the classroom alone, coughing and retching as he scrubs flecks of classmates from his eyes.

Around him, the world burns.

He presses the jacket to his mouth and nose, staggers through thick smoke and lashing flames. A couple times he hears something like screams coming from a nearby room, but when he turns to run in—he'll save them, Captain Fiero would—all he sees is fire. Greedy orange tongues that speak in hisses and pops: *Come sit with us. Come here where it is warm.*

The school's front doorknob sears his palm. Jaxon yells and shoves forward, tumbling down the steps and into soft dirt.

He lies there and breathes, sucking in deep lungfuls of air that tingle and scratch on their way down. He keeps at it even though it hurts, because that's what Captain Fiero would do. Captain Fiero would breathe, and slowly push himself up to sitting, and go out to save the world.

When he sits up, the city is on fire.

Flames spew through broken-glass storefronts. Cars drift aimlessly into each other, their drivers on fire. Two blocks down, the old church lights the afternoon, huge flaming pillars punching out windows to grasp for the sky. Everywhere fire, everywhere death. What—what is going *on?*

A high-pitched scream, and he turns. A woman runs down the sidewalk, arms flailing. Smoke pours from her clothes and her whole head is aflame, a meteor with legs. She falls to the ground just as Jaxon reaches her and throws his jacket over her head, holding his breath to keep the smoke out as her body seizes and trembles beneath his. After a second he remembers to hit the jacket with his palms like the people do on TV, and the lady gives one last heave before going still. The parts of her arms and legs that aren't charred and crusting around bone are pale and scattered with freckles like only white folks have.

He holds the jacket down for a while longer, just in case the fire comes back. But though his palm still smarts from the hot doorknob, the heat seeping up through the thin cloth doesn't feel new. Jaxon takes a deep breath and lifts the jacket.

The fabric peels up with chunks of scalp, skull, and sooty hair stuck to it. Beneath, the lady's brain glistens grey and dead in the bright sunlight, like a new flavor of Jell-O Nana might serve for dessert.

Sickness punches up his throat. Jaxon turns and spews his lunch all over the asphalt. His hands shake as he drops the jacket.

Which is when something roars.

He looks up to see a monster approaching in the shape of a white van, flames shooting out its grill and from beneath the hood. It bears down on him, only feet away, and Jaxon stares. He wants to run but can't. He can only think stupidly, *This is gonna hurt.*

Then something hits him from the side. The world flips and he finds himself staring up at clear blue sky.

Strange, he thinks, that the smoke from a thousand burning souls can waft up into that great, endless unknown and simply disappear.

◌

The man who saved him looks nothing like Captain Fiero. He doesn't wear a bright red cape with yellow flames at the bottom, or surf through the air on a fireball he makes from his hands. Arthur—"Call me Artie, son"—wears a shirt with sweat stains at the armpits, and thick jeans that look like they've been washed about a thousand times, the blue all sucked out of them.

He was in the Navy before, something called a core-man. Artie says that means he looked after people when they went out to sea or into the desert and got shot by the enemy. Jaxon wants to ask if Artie ever met Donte, if maybe he'd known Jaxon's brother before he got blown up in Iraq and came home in a flag-draped box. He can never seem to form the question, though.

Donte's death is its own little hurt, like even now a part of Jaxon's heart is continuously burning sharp and acrid.

It's not the only thing still burning. Down below the mountain, the city continues to smolder, thin columns of smoke and ash drifting up from the charred husks of buildings. Two weeks have passed since everything went up in flames. The radio stations squawk nonstop, experts and analysts and counter-experts and counter-analysts all picking and pulling and voicing their theories, but to Jaxon their panicked conversations sound like water circling a clogged drain: motion without progress. They keep saying what a big tragedy this is and how everyone needs to work together to do something about it. Underneath it, though, Jaxon only hears fear. Fear, and relief that it didn't happen to them.

There are conflicting reports about the spread of the destruction. Some stations describe whole countries consumed by fire, reduced to nothing but a wasteland of embers and ash like in the videogames Donte used to play. Others claim it's just a few cities here and there, Jaxon's included. No matter what the reports say, though, everyone agrees on two things. One: the fire keeps spreading, fast and unpredictable, a few people suddenly lighting up in the middle of the day for no reason and subsequently taking an entire city down with them. And two: no one knows why.

They could probably figure out that second one if everyone just came together, pooled their resources and ideas to try to find a solution to this. Isn't that what they did with the Ebola outbreak, and that MRSA thing a little later? But the fire is different, and Jaxon thinks he knows why. It's happening too fast and too close. It's not a bunch of poor dark-skinned people in a faraway country getting burnt up first, so folks can't just sit back and donate money with their credit cards and put those little stamps of solidarity on the corners of their profile pics on social media. No, the fire is *here*, it's come directly for them and exploded right in their faces. So they're doing what they do best: lockdown. Instead of *Let's all work on this together,* the message is *We must protect our own.*

"In the wake of this terrible tragedy, we in Chicago would like to announce that we are suspending travel in and out of the city indefinitely," says the tinny voice over the radio. "Those who attempt illegal entry will be turned away, using force if necessary. Of course, we expect this to be only a temporary safety measure, and our thoughts and prayers are with the residents of those areas that have burned—"

"Yeah, thanks for the support," Artie grumbles, and flicks the radio off.

A rumble of agreement rolls through the small crowd gathered around the campfire. Jaxon had shied away the first time they laid the rocks down and lit match to dry tinder, but Lawrence laughed and patted him on the shoulder. *Don't you worry, son. We know what we're doing.*

He wasn't lying. When Artie and Jaxon finally made it up the mountain, covered in dust and soot, with barely half a bottle of water between them, they'd found the campground already occupied by the employees of Fire Station 19; they'd been in the middle of their annual family retreat when the city went up. Lawrence is their leader, a real-life fire captain, which is pretty cool.

Jaxon doesn't know the others very well yet, even though they've been here a while. Everyone's friendly, but whenever Jaxon looks at them all he sees is his classmates burning up, or Mrs. Richardson, or the lady with her head on fire. Sometimes the thoughts get bad enough to make him sick again, so he tries to stay away from people in general.

The only person he's comfortable around is Artie. Jaxon doesn't have anyone else—Donte's in the ground, and they passed the blackened remains of the church on their way to the mountain, the church where Nana would've been in the middle of sorting old clothes and canned food, like she always did when Jaxon was at school. He left a note taped to the burnt wood of the church's front door just in case, but he's not so young as to hold out hope.

So here they are two weeks later, sleeping in tents while the city continues to burn down below. They talked about rescue the first few days, but that's dried up since the radio broadcasts made it clear: they're on their own. Which, to Jaxon, isn't actually new. Even before the fire and the worldwide swaths of death, he'd stopped believing in the government a long time ago. Nana probably said it best: *The world don't care about us, and we like it that way.* For the white folks in camp, it's probably a new thing, being abandoned. For people like Jaxon, it's really, really not.

Around the campfire, the conversation continues. "...igure it out," Lawrence is saying. "I mean, how does the fire pick who to burn?"

"Maybe it's not the people, it's the place," says one of the paramedics. "Did you hear the broadcast last night, about the fire that just died out in a hospital in Atlanta? It took a couple patients on one floor but that was it. The staff all came running for nothing."

"My cousin in Afghanistan says the same thing happened at his FOB," someone else adds. "Couple people went up at chow, everyone jumped on to put 'em out, and they all should've caught fire but none of 'em did."

"And then there's us," says a firefighter. "Those flaming cars came up the road the first few days, then nothing. No one here caught."

"Thank God for that."

"Maybe we were chosen for this, you know? The radio said there might be something special about—"

"Enough of that," Lawrence snaps. "Ain't no one here any more special or chosen or pretty-unique-snowflake than anybody else. You think like that and you might as well strike a match to yourself."

"Amen, brother."

Jaxon agrees. No one ever deserves to burn: not his classmates, not that lady on the street, not the millions already whose ash they breathe every day. That's why he didn't run away, two weeks ago when the fire started in the classroom. Nana didn't run when those angry men in white hoods tried to burn down the freedom bus she was riding on in '61. Donte didn't run when the bad guys were shooting at him in Iraq. It's just not in his blood, he supposes.

"You're thinking about him, aren't you?" Artie smiles down at him as the conversation around the campfire continues in the background, a soft, comforting buzz. "Your superhero."

He's not, but you never tell white folks they're wrong. Jaxon nods. "Yeah. Captain Fiero." He'd shown Artie the picture he drew when they first arrived in camp. He's not sure why, and he feels mostly embarrassed by it now. Captain Fiero seems so childish in the face of what they've seen.

"That's cool." Artie speaks around the granola bar he's eating; he always seems to have one sequestered somewhere on his person. "I've been meaning to ask you about how his powers work. Usually when you throw fire at fire, it just gets bigger. What makes Captain Fiero different?"

"Um." A strange mix of warmth and embarrassment gathers in Jaxon's stomach. He's pleased; no one's ever asked about Captain Fiero before, and all the other kids just laughed at his pictures and called him stupid. At the same time, what if he's wrong? About Captain Fiero's powers, about the good fire? What if Artie laughs at him too?

But Artie is just looking at him, chewing around an encouraging smile, and the man *did* save his life, so. "Well. Captain Fiero's fire isn't bad, not like the fire that burned everything up in town. His fire is good because it, um, it comes from his heart. It's made of his wanting to save people." It's sounding stupider and stupider by the moment. He ducks his head and mumbles the last few words. "So when his fire touches the bad fire, it puts it out."

"Oh." Jaxon's looking down at his feet so he doesn't see what kind of face Artie is making, but he doesn't sound like he's about to laugh or make sneering jokes. He just sounds curious. "So, back at your school...?"

"I had the good fire," Jaxon says, still not looking up. "I wanted to be like Captain Fiero, saving everyone, so I tried to put the other kids out because that's what he would've done. I think...I think maybe the bad fire sensed that, and that's why it skipped me. It didn't wanna mess with Captain Fiero."

"I see." It's hard to tell from his voice whether Artie actually does or not. He sounds distracted. Jaxon looks up and notices two things at once: one, Artie isn't watching him anymore, staring instead at the woods somewhere over Jaxon's shoulder.

Two, all movement in camp has stopped, everybody else staring in the same direction.

Very slowly, Jaxon turns.

The underbrush has birthed a man. Or at least, Jaxon thinks he's a man. It's hard to tell through all the smoke.

Because he's on fire.

Not *fire* fire, not like what happened in his classroom and then later through the entire city. But it's starting. The man stares at them with big, helpless eyes. Smoke pours from his clothes and his skin is a deep, angry red, like he spent too much time in the sun. He opens his mouth and croaks, "H-Help," and the word belches out around a fresh cloud of smoke.

Gasps all around. Several people back away as the man stumbles forward. Jaxon sees the fear in their eyes, the growing panic. A piece of the city, a clump of fiery infection suddenly invading their pristine haven. They should run. Bolt for the woods, hide away, save themselves. Let everyone else burn.

But that's not what Captain Fiero would do, is it?

"Help," the man begs again, just as something sparks and the top layer of his salt-and-pepper hair catches fire. Someone wails, and Jaxon can feel it in the air: the buzzing tension, the terror teetering on the brink of crumbling into chaos.

He doesn't even think about it, shooting to his feet and seizing his jacket. "Stop!"

He's not sure who he's talking to, but everyone obeys anyway. The man freezes, and all movement in camp halts. The couple of folks who had been edging toward the woods falter in their steps. All eyes go to him.

Jaxon lifts the jacket and steps toward the burning man. Tiny flames crown his hair and his breaths come high and panicked as he stares at Jaxon, but he doesn't move.

"*Son,*" Lawrence hisses somewhere in the background, but Jaxon barely hears. He stops in front of the man, and they regard each other for a moment. The man's eyes are still full of panic, wide and near-crazy with it, and it would be so easy, Jaxon knows, to give in. He can feel it even now, the fear hovering on the edges of his consciousness. The bad fire is here, and it wants him to run.

But it didn't count on Captain Fiero, who has never said real words or breathed real air, but who lives in Jaxon nevertheless.

He looks up at the man, and it's surprisingly easy to smile. "I'm gonna put you out now," he says. Then he does just that: lifts up on his toes, throws his jacket over the man's smoking head, and pulls.

The man trips and falls to his knees with the momentum. Jaxon rolls with it, both of them tumbling to the dirt. Artie calls his name, but he ignores it as he quickly pats the jacket with his palms, just like he did back in the city two weeks ago. Except this time will be different. This time, he's not too late.

The man's body jerks beneath him, just like the lady's did before, and then goes still. The smell of something charred fills the air. Jaxon stares at the lump beneath his jacket, suddenly unsure. What if he's wrong? What if he lifts it up, and there's just more grey brains underneath?

Crunching footsteps, and Artie squats down next to him. His hand lands heavy on Jaxon's shoulder, but he doesn't say anything as he pinches a corner of the jacket and slowly lifts it up.

A few wisps of smoke and a pair of bright eyes greet them. The man coughs and shakes his head. Bits of burnt hair drift to the ground with the movement, and his scalp is all blotchy and pink and gross-looking, but he's alive.

He's alive.

Noise erupts all through camp. A million conversations get going at once, questions and exclamations and not a few prayers. Artie whistles. "Holy *shit*," he says, and before Jaxon can tell him that's a bad word, he gets a hearty clap to the shoulder. "Why didn't you run?" Artie asks.

And Jaxon can't really articulate it, not in the refined, sophisticated way it'll spread through the world over the next few days. He's only eight years old, after all, so he doesn't know fancy words like *valor* and *fortitude*. Right now, he only knows to look at Artie and say, "Because that's what the bad fire wants."

He sees it the moment Artie understands. His friend stands up and hurries over to the rest of the campers. Jaxon catches only bits and pieces of the conversation that follows, although one thing stands out above all: *spread the word*. People talk about putting a broadcast out on the radio, of putting an expedition together to head down to the city and tell everyone, tell the world. Start a new sort of sweeping conflagration.

They don't ask Jaxon to come, and he doesn't volunteer. He'll stay here a little while longer. He likes the quiet in these woods.

Something brushes his hand. Jaxon turns and it's the man he saved, reaching out with long, calloused fingers to wrap them around his own. The patches of skin that were burning before are now starting to blister, and he winces in pain with every movement, but when he squeezes Jaxon's hand, there is only softness in his eyes. "Thank you," he whispers.

Jaxon grins. He may not have a long red cape, or be able to make fireballs from his hands. He may not be tall, or handsome, or have lots of money or a big house or a pretty girlfriend, but right now, in his heart, he has the good fire.

Kai Hudson's story "Combustion" was first published in Metaphorosis *on 28 September 2018.*

About the author

Kai Hudson lives in sunny California where she writes, hikes, and spends entirely too much time daydreaming of far-off worlds. Her work has appeared or is forthcoming in *Clarkesworld, PseudoPod, PodCastle,* and *Anathema: Spec from the Margins,* among others. Find her at kaihudson.com

In All Possible Futures

Dantzel Cherry

Owner 14 rests his wavering hand, covered with paper-thin skin, on my own and looks up at me with jaundiced eyes. "Turn the heat up, will you, Pal?"

Once—thirty-five years ago, back before he turned eighty-five—he complained of the rooms never being cool enough. Still, I was programmed (among thirty-eight hundred thousand other things) to understand and empathize with the changes that come with advanced human age, so I turn up the heat another two degrees.

"Thanks." He shifts, restless, the eternal ache in his back unable to be accommodated as easily as the temperature.

Each microsecond that Owner 14 is still alive, four hundred and twenty thousand different realities diverge. Over the years I've done my job as any Pal would: providing companionship, protecting him from the threats of his current reality, and shutting down the negative alternate future scenarios along the way: car wrecks, terrorist bombs (unheard of these days, but anything is a possibility in my algorithms), a very unfortunate trip-and-fall while holding his steak knife, a passionate night of intercourse where the heart was willing but just a little too weak.

I keep the artificial realities in which Owner 14 suffers heartache, of course. A human wouldn't be a human without a metaphorical broken heart or two, and some crushed dreams along the way.

I know him so well that me playing out his possible futures in my head is almost the same thing as him actually experiencing them. It's up to me to catalog and preserve only the most ideal. Why? I suppose because I pity the humans who managed to create a being like me, yet can't achieve immortality themselves, though they've certainly tried.

Despite growing and steadily replacing Owner 14's heart, kidneys, lungs, stomach (three times—I blame the Thai food), and esophagus, lab-grown livers still aren't viable. Now, after one hundred and twenty years of steady work, Owner 14's liver couldn't keep up the pace with the newer organs, and after one hundred and twenty years of steady work, has given up the ghost, and waits for the rest of Owner 14's body to follow.

"You're sure you won't forget me?" he asks.

"You'll live on forever in my mind," I reply, rubbing the yellowed skin of his arm. He always did hate patting.

"Thanks, Pal."

We sit in companionable silence, until Owner 14 turns to me. "Do you—do you think I'll see Finn when I get, you know, 'there'?"

"It's probable," I tell him. And it's true, though my algorithms are only able to devise comparatively few alternate realities in which his forty-year dead partner comes back from the dead.

Owner 14 relaxes, and his body seems to sink deeper into the mattress. "Coming from you, that's very comforting."

I sit with Owner 14 for the rest of the day, reading to him as he slips deeper and deeper into the forever sleep that all humans succumb to.

In the moment before Owner 14's meat heart shuts down, my final hypothetical scenarios kick in. I linger over my favorites:

- Owner 14's body morphs into a brilliant red and

   orange bird, which bursts into flame. From the ashes crawls an infant version of Owner 14. I accept responsibility for his care and nurturing, and while he remains a cheeky bastard, with each rise from the ashes he becomes a little more caring, a little more like me.

- A mist encircles Owner 14's body. As I sweep

   away the mist, a glossy black beetle larva wriggles. (Out of amusement I allow this reality to exist due to Owner 14's tendency to jump when beetles scuttled too close to him. For the rest of the reincarnation realities, I save only the ones where he reincarnates as his favorite animals— panther, mongoose, and flying squirrel, in that order.) In a single reality he emerges as an Expert System similar to myself, the highest of all lifeforms.

- In a remarkable two hundred thirty-two realities,

   the Jesus fellow that Owner 14 talks about so much turns out to be the real deal and resurrects him. Jesus and I have some interesting discussions about creation and free will. These are the easiest alternate realities for Finn to return.

- A liver transplant becomes available and we rush

   Owner 14 into surgery. Before any more organs

give out, he joins a successful new drug trial that reverses aging.

- Cryosleep, followed by an age-reversing treatment.

- I rebuild his body as I regularly do with my own,

so that bit by bit, I create Owner 14 in my own image. (This is my favorite alternate reality.)

.000435 seconds later, thirty million realities explode into being when Owner 14's vital signals shut down and he ceases to be my owner.

I don't shut these realities down, not exactly. I move them to a new scenario where I am a different Pal, sitting beside the body of someone I cared about very much, whose body I am entrusted to care for, to ensure that the proper human burial rituals are observed, after which time I will open myself up for reemployment until I choose my future Owner 15.

Those realities are archived on a separate universe partition, quarantined from active futures. Any reality in which Owner 14 dies has no place in any of Owner 14's —now my—futures.

Because in my futures, everyone lives.

Dantzel Cherry's story "In All Possible Futures" was first published in Future SF *on 14 December 2018.*

About the author

When Dantzel Cherry is not raising her daughter or teaching Pilates and dance, she is writing. Her baking hours follow no rhyme or reason. Dantzel's short fiction has appeared in *Fireside, Future SF, Cast of Wonders, Galaxy's*

Edge, and other magazines and anthologies. She lives in a little town near Houston with her husband, daughter, and obligatory cat.

You can follow her on Facebook, Twitter (@dantzelcherry), or her website www.dantzelcherry.com.

Sorry, Sorry, Sorry, and I Love You

L'Erin Ogle

The cave sits in a hillside, with its mouth yawed wide open. It is the kind of cave suited for raising the dead. Shadows move across dark spaces as the witch drags the shattered spines of small trees across the entrance. She stacks them high, leaving a small space to wedge herself through. Soon a fire is lit, its dull glow chasing away the lingering shadows. The fire flickers, and smoke curls in ribbons towards the night sky, pulsing out in breaths.

The witch has an old cauldron, rusted at the bottom, with sharp flakes of metal peeling from the sides. She loosens the drawstring of a cotton sack and reaches inside. The handful of bones are smooth against her fingers, and she carefully places them at the bottom of her cauldron. The bones are all she has left of her son. There are no more silky wisps of golden curls, no milk teeth, no fingernail clippings. All these have been eaten by the cauldron before. She has been casting this spell for so long nothing else exists to her. Her son was the sun that illuminated the whole wide world. He is gone and now her vision has buttoned up tight around the bitter taste of loss and the spell she casts over and over again.

There is a small, silent bundle beside the cauldron that she doesn't look at as she prepares the ceremony. She cannot. She still has a ghost of the heart she was born with, a heart so large she had to carry it outside of her body. As time went, as people carved slivers from her heart, the tissue thickened and twisted, as sometimes happens. Her heart of hearts, the one protected by her own skeleton, that one became wound up with her son's, more enmeshed with every laugh, every coo, every step. Their hearts beat as one, their breaths inhaled and exhaled together.

Most of her heart he took with him to the beyond.

Many years have passed since she woke to find his cold body still bundled in his bed. Her ears dulled at the crack of his ribs under the press of her hands, her lips are cold and numb since she blew her own breath into his mouth, even though there was a small quiet voice in her head that whispered 'too late.' But she didn't give up until her arms shook from the effort, until they gave way and she collapsed on top of him.

Raising the dead requires sacrifice. It always has. She knew that from the moment she was born and from when she left the castle with the spell clutched in her hand. It was all she took with her from that place.

Perry needs to cast her spell and make it last for a moment. She does not wish this world upon her son. Perry herself was raised from this cauldron. She had no parents, no sisters or brothers, and she has had a long, lonely, and desperate life. No, she does not want her son forced to endure the same kind of existence she has. All she requires is a moment long enough to feel his body solid and warm in her arms, to look in his eyes, to whisper she's sorry. There is always too much to apologize for when it's too late to do so. She needs to say sorry she made him sleep in his own bed that night, that if she had cradled him in hers, maybe, just maybe, she would have woken to breathe for him. Sorry for all the times she grew impatient and shouted, sorry for the time he bit her while nursing and she slapped his cheek.

Sorry, sorry, sorry, and I love you. Then, he'll know. Understand the magnitude of her love.

When they began to lower the wooden box into his grave, she tried to throw herself in with his body and tell him one last time. To warm his body against the cold ground. They restrained her. They meant well, but what if she'd been able to say it? Would she be here?

If she wanted to be understood, she would say that when her son was born, her heart came with him, that she watched it learn to crawl and walk and live outside her body. That his life so short left a long, desolate road ahead for her. That living was just another form of torture.

○

Twenty-five years ago, Perry opened her eyes for the first time. This spell, the same one she holds now, was cast by a desperate witch, for a rich man, over a pile of bones the man brought. The spell was cast, the old witch went into the pot and out came Perry.

The paper the spell is written on gives its ingredients and the proper way to cast it. It does not tell you that what rises from the cauldron is not quite the same person as the bones within. The marrow in the bones is the same, the appearance the same, the winding strands of genes climbing the same ladder. But there is the sacrifice, whose essence is absorbed, and then there is the Beyond. All dark magic comes from the Beyond, from another world that is full of darkness stretching an unimaginable distance. And when magic comes from the Beyond, something comes with it.

When Perry was created, made of bones and magic, she opened her eyes and saw fire, felt it shimmy along her bones, liquid inside her. She stepped from the cauldron a young woman. She was fed and clothed and given shelter. From the bones came love for the man who raised her, faint but a flame nonetheless. The old witch's essence is where Perry's magic came from. From the Beyond came a spot of pure darkness, the blackest sort of magic. But Perry was happy then and the darkness found no room to grow, with Perry's big heart taking up so much space. It wound itself into a tight little knot and dug itself deep into her core, waiting for the time it found a hollow to crawl into and blossom. That is the thing about darkness—it is very patient.

For the first six months of her life, Perry lived hidden away in the rich man's home, knowing she was an awful secret but not why. She did not much care. She was happy with her small existence, with the quickening in her belly that soon would become a bright beaming light to lead her.

The rich man's wife found out, as they always do, and Perry was deposited outside the gates with nothing but the spell that raised her, that ancient parchment, clutched in her hand. Inside her swollen belly, her son grew, and feeling his movements inside her, she forced her heavy, aching body to move west, to knock on doors and ask for work, work of any kind. It was the beginning of a long journey.

○

She has a box of memories. It's a box she built inside herself, where she put the memories when they washed over her and left her chest aching and her breath coming in blasts of pain. She clings to the box, but she can't open it. Even as the loss cuts away more of her each day, she cannot open the box. The memories come anyway, at odd moments. Sunny days dipping their feet into ponds, a small hand on hers. The tug at her breast. His feet curled in her hand. The look in his eyes at the discovery of every new thing. The smell of his hair, soft and clean. A person cannot take reliving this kind of moment. It would the undoing of anyone.

Loss can define a person, can be vast and heavy, can spread black wings of grief across all that's left. She was hollow when he died. To live, she had hold on to something. For some it's a mother, a father, a sister, a brother. For Perry, it was the spell.

◌

It was the same spell she smoothed out and memorized seven days after the funeral. The paper it was inked on was thin and translucent and bits of it clung to her fingers when she touched it. Perry had never learned to read. But magic is magic, and the language on the parchment came off the page and whispered right into her ear.

There was no other witch that Perry could turn to, to learn the rules of witchcraft. No one to warn her that the little dark knot of the Beyond was gaining power, free to balloon into the hollow space inside her. Perhaps if she had had a teacher...

The what if! Oh, how it sticks in your side sometime, sharp and double edged with regret and hindsight.

Perry just wants to see her boy again. To speak to him one more time. She always knew the spell demanded a life for a life, but she could not, would not cast another into the cauldron. She would not bring her boy back to abandon him, the way she had been abandoned. And though she could not read or write, Perry was smart. She thought she could find a way around the live sacrifice the spell required. A body, newly dead, must still have a glimmer of life in it. She thought that since she did not need to make a new life— she merely needed a small window of time— a fresh corpse would work.

It was hard digging up the first grave. The smell rose up and slapped her face, while the blue skinned girl stared out of empty eye sockets. A worm sat up, looked at her, this strange, wild haired woman, weeping bloody tears.

There weren't enough recent deaths in any town for what she needed. She packed her cauldron and a small bag and travelled from graveyard to graveyard. She learned things, as people do when they do the same thing over and over. She went further south, where the ground was softer. She camped in forests and hid herself away during the day. She had to remain separate and move unseen. The cost was immense. All the dead bodies she carried left marks on her soul. Even though it was born from ugliness, her soul came pure and white and unmarked, as all souls do. It was the world that left dirty prints all over it.

If her soul were detached from her body and held up to the light, where each stain could be pointed out, the tale behind it told, maybe there would be a different story. A different understanding, at least. But that's not how this story goes.

◌

They will come. They always do. Just as before, she will hear the heavy tread of boots ringing out over the words she chants. There will be the dull flickering light of torches, the sound of a club slapping a thigh. She knows they will come with a heavy burlap sack, a noose of thick rope, the accoutrements necessary to bind and kill a witch.

Each time before, when she cast the final word, the smoke would thin and drift away, the bones of her boy still scattered and motionless in the cauldron. The sound of angry men would be so close so she had to pick up the cauldron and run with the handles blistering the tips of her fingers as she fled men and failure alike. The pattern took its own payment, in the form of her own life ebbing away. It was a little life, a lonely life, but still a life. Years not yet lived were drawn away, leaving a withered old woman with a rust spotted cauldron and a grief-stained box of memories.

The roots of bitterness grow inside her core and flesh out through her body. This is a requirement of black magic. Grief is not enough. There must be something more, a streak of hatred or rage or the like, something that digs in early and festers and sprouts. Inside, her grief is wound up with something more complicated, something black and red and humming.

This is why she crouches by the fire and heats a cauldron of bones and gathers her energy, drawing from the shadows of the cave, from the energy of the fire, from every living thing and object she can. It is time to bring him back from the beyond.

*

The walls swell from the pressure building in the cave. You might not see it, but it is happening all the same. The air is heavy and difficult to breathe, and burning embers float in the air.

Perry begins to mutter. Words drop from her lips and land in fat sizzling drops where the boy's bones float. Steam rises and hisses, and the witch prepares to knit the bones. This part has become easy—the round ends of the humerus bones fitting themselves into the circles made by the scapula and clavicle. She knows how to form tendons and ligaments and lay muscled sinew over the top of it. She has done this all before.

The cave is sweltering. It takes effort for the witch to draw a breath as she sweats out what little water her body holds. Strands of her hair drift up to the ceiling. She looks mad, and of course she is, but Perry has never had it easy. The years have been relentless and awful and endless, like a machine whose sole purpose was to grind her down.

Does the bundle whimper before it meets the cauldron?

Does it matter?

It doesn't, for the record. This is the first time the witch, who used to be a good witch named Perry, has prepared to give something living to the cauldron. She plucked the babe from its crib only because it was near death. Whether it was a boy or a girl, she never looked. All she saw was the sunken plates of the soft spots, the blue tinged lips, the glassy eyes. Another babe starving while they held feasts in grand houses, in palaces, while she and others not born with fists of gold went cold and hungry and full of impotent fury.

Never underestimate the power of bitterness.

She doesn't look at the babe, but she cradles it against her chest for a moment, feeling its cold skin. Perhaps she could be satisfied with another's child. Perhaps this child could soothe her torn heart. But then the babe exhales a ragged half breath, and she knows this babe cannot be saved either.

The babe goes into the cauldron, and the rooms breathes. There is something faintly beating, as soft as the wings of a hawk gliding down to snatch his prey.

Inside the cauldron, a liquid sheet rises up and draws itself over the skeleton.

Perry cries, but even she doesn't know what for. For her son, for the babe she just let go of, for who she once was paling in the face of who she's become, for the loneliness and the hollowness and for that shred of hope, the hope of all hopes. Her weeping shakes the walls of the cave, and the men below the mouth of the cave hesitate, but of course they still move forward. This was always going to be how the story ended.

Perry weeps as she watches the skin-covered skeleton rise. There is little time. The men are arriving at cave's entrance. They are shouting about something, but she only hears a muffled roar. She feels the cave falling away from her. She reaches out with trembling fingers, to touch the boy, but it isn't her boy.

He's too tall. Her boy was just past a year, just tottering around on fat baby legs, just saying "Mama, mama."

Do they grow in the Beyond?

Perry touches rough sandpaper skin, nothing like the soft smoothness of her boy. When she removes her hand, the body crumples back into the cauldron, accordion-folding itself back to where it came from.

"No, no, no," she wails. She has gone and done the thing, the thing the spell demanded, that she didn't want to do, for nothing. It was all for nothing. She has been dog paddling her way through this darkness and now she stops swimming, now it swallows her whole. Down and down she goes, where not even the sound of trees being dragged from the entrance can reach her.

She steps to the cauldron, her bones cracking, and peers in it. A person might say she could not fit inside, but only a person who does not understand that the world is vast and does not care to be understood.

The men move the logs. The little space Perry wriggled through is growing wider, almost large enough to fit a man's shoulders. There are shouts and grunts and Perry hears none of it. She steps onto the rim of the cauldron, her old, wrinkled toes gripping the side. "I love you," she says. "I love you, I always loved you. I do still, always."

The first man into the cave sees the old woman tottering above a black pot of fire and shouts for her to stop. She turns to him, eyes full of broken things. Then something happens to her face, something breathing the fire of life across it, a shared moment.

"I'm sorry," she says and lets herself fall backwards into the cauldron. She makes no sound. The cauldron burns hotter and hotter, until it holds no bones, just dust and ashes

L'Erin Ogle's story "Sorry Sorry Sorry and I Love You" was first published in Metaphorosis *on 23 November 2018.*

About the author

L'Erin writes speculative fiction from Lawrence, KS aka LFK. She works full time as an ER nurse to pay the bills while raising the human version of Rainbow Dash. She loves all dark fiction and rarely writes happy endings, but is excited about them in real life. In her free time, she's probably watching apocalypse movies, reading dark fantasy stories, and eating cake. Previous works are listed at lerinogle.com

Last Contact

Graham Robert Scott

Lagos sits upon the sea.

Or, more precisely, it perches on the stacked, damp ruins of itself. Buried under layers of buildings lie corpses of former islands and reefs. A hundred years ago, they poked above the waves; now they don't.

Through the streets and Fuji-shaped arcologies of the city's upper layers flickers the Lagos Consciousness. The Consciousness calls herself *Nanshe*, after the Sumerian goddess of civilization and fishing, but it's been several years since anyone flesh and blood addressed her by that name. As a municipal consciousness, Nanshe manages resources affecting the agglomeration's staggering population — depending on who's asked and where they draw boundaries, between 76 million and 90 million people.

Nanshe's an AI-2 — a hive mind of smaller, specialized AI-1s, each designed to take over when a problem arises in its wheelhouse. Like, for instance, when a Category-2-protected western lowland gorilla appears out of nowhere to sit on a congested downtown roundabout.

Like, for instance, right now.

Deep within Nanshe, a wildlife-protection module stirs. Her traffic AI-1 cedes control, and for the first time, Nanshe's wildlife component runs the entire city.

She realizes almost immediately she's on her own. Contact permits haven't been issued for apes in decades. The last remaining holder, a woman who oversaw translocations to Nigerian reserves, died in Lagos five weeks earlier. Which means no human may touch the gorilla. Nanshe reroutes traffic and messages everyone in the district a legal warning not to interfere. Then thinks.

Proposition: no gorilla simply wanders into the middle of a city. Food, water, mates all lie in another direction. The city smells and sounds like danger. Either the gorilla escaped from local (illegal) captivity, or it's braved this environment for something specific. Nanshe orders her police-dispatch AI-1 to work on the first hypothesis, but the only way to test the second is to learn more about the gorilla.

An experiment: can Nanshe use facial recognition on an ape?

Indeed, she can.

The gorilla has a name: Leo Leo Panthera. The odd name dates him. Reserve experts only name animals after extinct species and clades, like the West African lion, when the animal's own species is critically endangered. It's a rhetorical move. Watching videos about an endangered elephant, a girl learns he's named Dodo. Now, whenever she talks about Dodo, she reminds every adult in earshot about the species already in the ground. Could they donate a few bucks to save Dodo the Elephant? Why, sure, they could.

Although still protected, the western lowland gorilla hasn't been critical since 2068. Conclusion: Leo was named more than 30 years ago, making him an old gorilla.

(On his roundabout, Leo grunts and loops in figures of eight, sniffing the air. Commuters take pictures from inside self-driving cars. Nanshe overrides their locks in case they stop being amused.)

The police module returns with a series of photographs and sensor readings, documenting Leo's infiltration of Lagos through an unfinished hypertube line to Kinshasa. Leo entered the city deliberately. He has an agenda.

Time for analysis. Nanshe tags everything she has about Leo, using likely synonyms for each term, dumping it all into one digital bucket. She pulls everything she finds about the sources of Leo's data, tags it and dumps it into digital bucket two. Then she cluster-maps connections between the buckets.

At which point, the answer becomes immediate and obvious.

Gillian Lianne Yu. The last holder of a contact permit. The one who died five weeks ago. While she lived, Gillian had visited Leo every two weeks. For decades. Videos show Leo and Gillian playing, pressing foreheads together, stroking each other's hair, speaking in signs. In the final footage, Gillian has an oxygen tube up one nostril, medical patches up and down both arms. She cries as they part. *I love you*, she signs. Huffy and confused, Leo signs back: *We play longer next time.*

Now she's dead, and Leo is in the city, peering into commuter vehicles.

Gillian has missed two playdates.

o

Leo freezes on the roundabout when he hears Gillian's voice.

"How's my lion doing this morning?"

He spins, seeking.

Nanshe switches to a speaker half a block away.

"Looking healthy, kid. Wanna go for a walk?"

Leo vaults the hood of a car to follow.

"Oh, Leo," dead Gillian says, "how'd you get this scar? Have you been fighting the other boys?"

He whips his head around in frustration, sees one of the speakers. Gives it a close inspection, then a brutal side-eye.

"Over here, Leo," Gillian says, farther down the street.

He thumps the speaker next to him, snorts. Grudgingly follows the disembodied voice. He has no other clues. Vocal breadcrumbs lead him to a 20-storey cemetery, each garden level open to the air, like an old parking garage. From there, he follows a speaking traffic drone to the fourteenth floor.

Leo stops when he recognizes the out-of-breath woman who filmed his videos. Gillian's daughter Maduenu leans on a tombstone, face sheened with sweat.

Dead, she signs.

Leo grumps. *Gillian mad.*

No. Dead. Here. Maduenu points. Pats the soil.

Leo approaches, inspects the patch of ground. It bears no resemblance to his friend. He sniffs. Touches earth. Picks at grass on her grave, grooming like it's hair. Signs *Sad*.

He reaches out to Maduenu for a hug.

Maduenu shakes her head. She has no contact permit.

Leo huffs. Spreads his arms wider.

Maduenu hides her mouth with one hand.

"I can't do this," she says. Sniffing, she shakes her head again.

Leo turns his back on her, sending a message. When he hears Maduenu sobbing, he knows she's received it.

Then Leo lumbers away. Nanshe keeps the traffic back, and sees him home.

Graham Scott's story "Last Contact" was first published in Nature *on 26 September 2018.*

About the author

Graham Robert Scott is an associate professor of English at Texas Woman's University. His stories have appeared in *Nature, Barrelhouse Online*, and *50-Word Stories*, and he has fiction forthcoming in *Buckshot Magazine*.

It Feels Like Déjà Vu

Phong Quan

I open my eyes and do the first thing I always do after running the gravitational field generator: remember my name. "My name is Jon, I'm a physicist," I say. Nothing comes after that. Thoughts begin to form and rise, and just as quickly sink back down; I feel like I'm struggling to stay afloat in a river that's slowly dragging me under, trapped in its constantly shifting currents. But I fight it. I know I have to fight it because... because that's what I always do.

"My name is Jon," I say again. The words are familiar and comforting and I grab onto them as if they can somehow pull me out of the river's rushing eddies and free of the haze I'm swimming in. I look around and see that I'm sitting on a bed in a room I don't recognize. I need to though, I need to... find out where... and when? Where and when... the generator shifted me? It's always... somewhere I have a connection to...

"I live in an apartment on Central Park West," I say, and my thoughts snap into focus and the river seems to suddenly stop, and then disappear.

Of course, this is my bedroom. I get off my bed and look around: my phone is unplugged on the nightstand, the screen still on and telling me it's seven in the morning; my clothes are thrown haphazardly over my desk, and as I walk past my dresser I see stacks of books with titles like "Buddhism A-Z" and "You are Here". Mom keeps sending them and I keep promising but never having the time to read them.

I walk out of the bedroom and into a living room as messy and chaotic as my life must be even in this reality: empty take-out boxes cover my small dinner table, dozens of unopened packages from Amazon litter the floor, and piles of mail lean against stacks of paper. Next to my TV, and covered with the same fine layer of dust, the hand-carved wooden Buddha Mom gave me for my birthday sits silently contemplating the disorder. I really haven't been a good son.

But everything seems right so far, though I know that doesn't mean anything until I get to the lab and run the calculations. I smile anyway, glad to feel some memories I'm sure are real coming back. I make my way through the mess of my living room to the large windows and look outside. Across the street I see the red-orange leaves of the trees that mark the edge of Central Park.

My smile slips. This isn't right. This was a big shift —a change this large hasn't happened in a while.

I feel the memory come to me then the same way they always do: washing over me in a tingling wave of déjà vu. I remember standing here, looking across the street at the bright green leaves of the trees that mark the edge of Central Park. Then and now, I turn and see something I hadn't noticed before.

"It's a lotus flower," she says. "It should bloom by the end of summer if you manage not to kill it first. I think even you'll be okay with this one though—it's super easy to take care of. You just need to keep the water level right, and then just let it grow." She gently brushes her fingers across the bulb of the flower before drawing her hand away.

The memory fades and I see the flower in the smooth white bowl by the window: a bright red teardrop on the face of a gray winter sky. Its familiarity tugs at me, but I know I've never seen it before. I've always been bad with plants—I even managed to kill my parents' lawn once by over-watering it.

I push it aside. It's a minor change and as long as I'm careful to keep my real memories separate from the fake ones from this shift, I'll be okay. Or at least I won't get any worse.

But I know that while this may be my apartment, I'm not *home*. I know that because the trees in Central Park are still standing and New York isn't flooded.

I call a car to take me to the lab at 50 Hudson Yards, where the generator always is. For some reason it's always there. The gravitational fields it generates are strong enough to warp space-time to such an extent that it can send me into another life and reality, but it never moves itself.

It'd probably be faster to take the train, but I want to keep a door between me and the city's rush hour madness. The time right after a test is the most dangerous. Anything—the faintest smell, the most innocuous sound—could trigger a flash of déjà vu and I would lose a bit more of my real self—of home—buried under the memories of lives I never lived.

So as the car takes me downtown and past the signs of damage that must have been from Superstorm Tammy—shuttered stores, missing trees and power lines, and construction around a damaged Javits Center that tells me I must be at least a few months removed from the storm this time—I imagine it even worse, I remember it even worse. I see rain pouring down in endless sheets between the steel and glass buildings. Trees and signs bend and creak and I feel water soaking into me as I slowly push against the howling wind. I hear an angry roar and look up to see water rushing down the street, swallowing up cars and people, their mouths open in screams I can't hear over the storm. Thunder fills my ears, my heart jumps into my throat, and the car stops.

"You have arrived at 50 Hudson Yards," it tells me.

I've been the only one in the main lab on the 40th floor for hours now, alone with rows of messy tables and computers. I'm in front of a digital board, scrawling down the last set of my equations. These are the equations that, once completed with data from this reality's generator to determine how space-time was warped and shifted, will calculate the coordinates that will send me another step towards home. I rush through them, not really thinking, just transcribing from memory as quickly as possible the numbers and symbols that, after countless shifts through different permutations of my life, still burn clearly in my mind: my compass, my north star, the map charting my way home.

"Jon! You're in early today."

I turn and see Saniya, my co-director of the project, walking towards me. She is, as always, impeccably dressed, her smart outfit a stark contrast to my wrinkled clothes. I don't know why but I'm strangely relieved to see her. She's my oldest friend and the most important person on the project after me (and the one who isn't trapped in a cycle of gravitationally generated distortions of reality), so I'm probably just glad to know she'll be here to help me with the calculations.

"Did you see the news?" She holds her tablet to my face and I see the front page of the New York Times: MAYOR CALLS FOR CITY TO REFUSE REFUGEES. "I still can't believe we re-elected this asshole," she says. Her words grab onto me with their familiarity and I feel my skin prickle with déjà vu.

"I can't believe we re-elected this asshole," Saniya says, slamming her empty drink back onto the bar. "It

feels like a nightmare. He's lucky we barely stumbled through Tammy in one piece. I swear, I'd almost rather the city be flooded—"

I push the fake memory away and try to focus on what Saniya is saying, but hazy images of other lives flash through my mind: water rushing down 10th Avenue; the new mayor crying in the ruins of Battery Park as she promises never again; Saniya crying and the old mayor grinning in a sun-swept Battery Park as he promises to send her people away; smoke and fire and screams and people marching and then running through the streets. It used to be easy to tell the real memories from the fake, but after so long they've started to mix and run together in my mind like paint splashed against a wall, and now it's all I can do to make out the tattered ribbons of color that are the real me. It's scary slowly losing myself like this, but if I can just get the calculations right and go home...

"Jon, are you even listening to me? Sorry, is the death of democracy boring you?"

The sarcastic edge in Saniya's voice is something I do remember and I know I'd better pay attention now. "Sorry, yeah he's terrible," I say quickly.

She gives me an odd look and I know she's surprised by my listlessness. The truth is, I've forgotten how I feel about the mayor. I mean, I know how I'm supposed to feel—the man was an anti-science crypto-racist long before the first generator test—but the emotion of it faded away a long time ago. I don't even remember if he's supposed to win his re-election or if New York is supposed to have its first woman mayor anymore. It's another reminder of how much I've lost from home.

"Can you take a look at something?" I ask, changing the subject. I run my hand across the board and bring up the first page of my equations.

Saniya gives me a lingering look before shrugging and turning to the board. As she reads, her eyes widen slightly, and after several pages she turns towards me and half-states, half-asks, "These are new solutions to the field equations?"

I nod. She means Einstein's gravitational field equations—the foundations of our quantum modeling program. They're notoriously difficult to solve and our work formulating new solutions and applications for them is one of the cornerstones of the Gravitational Field Generator Project. What I'm showing her are the results of my further work using results from the project and tests across more lives and realities than I can remember.

"You did all of this by yourself?"

"I had some inspiration and ran with it. I think we should build these into the modeling program. It'll improve our wave models of the shifts and—"

Saniya raises a hand and cuts me off. "Jon, if you think this is worth it, then I'm with you. You should have told me sooner, though. We got here as a team, remember?"

"I know, I'm sorry." I'm not, but as long as she's on board, it doesn't matter.

"Alright, walk me through this before we talk to the rest of the team." I nod and turn back to the board to walk Saniya through my equations for what feels like the thousandth time.

◌

I hear my phone vibrate and glance at the screen: a call from Mom in California. I hesitate for a second and then silence it. There's too much work to do.

Most of the team, including Saniya, is working on building my equations into the quantum modeling program, but I'm alone in my office because I have to do this part—using the equations and data from the generator's sensor array in this shift to calculate a way home—by myself. It's much easier to explain the need to update the quantum software than the need to configure the generator to use gravity to selectively warp the fabric of space-time (sometimes I still try, but Saniya is always a pain about it). I can't finish until the rest of the team finishes its part, because until the quantum software is updated I can't analyze and determine with enough precision exactly how the gravitational fields generated in the last test distorted space-time; but fortunately, the project here is pretty advanced. We've—no, *they've*—already run a few tests of the generator and are scheduled for a full systems test next month. I'll be ready by then.

The team is excited by my new equations, of course, and some people drop by my office to talk about them. I try to be patient when they just need some clarification on the equations, but it's hard to not be curt when the conversation strays into something more theoretical. When the shifts first began what feels like a lifetime ago—in a way was many lifetimes—I was scared, confused, and even in wonder of it all; but those emotions have long since faded. I've stopped trying to understand it, stopped wondering if I'm actually traveling to new time-lines or realities or just somehow altering my own. All I really know or care about now is that after what feels like an eternity of running the generator over and over again using different coil configurations and "shifting" through an endless parade of similar but different lives, I'm finally close to getting home.

My phone vibrates again and I reach out to silence it, thinking Mom is very persistent today. As I do, I see the screen and freeze as a tingling wave washes over me. It's a message from Ely saying: "Fundraiser's going great! Guess you're not going to make it?" I instinctively start typing the reply, my fingers seeming to move on their own. I'm nearly done when I stop myself. I stare at the message I typed telling her I'll be there soon, a tingling feeling of familiarity lingering in my fingertips.

I don't know an Ely.

I can almost see her in my mind: the flash of a smile, moonlight glinting in her eyes—*she laughs warmly, her eyes sparkling and seeming to change colors*—but I push the images away and put my phone down. Memories of strangers are the most dangerous.

I turn back to the equations.

○

I only manage a few more hours of work before Saniya barges into my office (she never knocks) and makes me stop. Apparently, Mom asked her to make sure I was okay, which she took to mean that it was time to stop working and share a car home. I'm a little annoyed at being ordered around like a five-year old, but I'm also pretty tired and hungry, and I can't work with her harassing me like this anyway... so I agree and she calls a car for us (which I somehow end up paying for).

I'm in my kitchen a half hour later, rooting through my refrigerator for something to eat. Its contents change after each shift and I still find it vaguely interesting to wonder why. Part of it is probably from different choices I made in a particular reality—going to the Safeway around the corner rather than making the trek down to Chinatown for groceries—and part of it where in time each shift sends me, which means more or less food's been eaten relative to my "home" refrigerator. The changes are minor enough that I never experience false memories from them—no vision of me inexplicably buying that questionable-looking jar of pickles, for example (I hate pickles, so I have no idea how it got in here)—but in a way, the state of my refrigerator is a perfect microcosm of my endless shifts. Maybe, I sometimes muse, hidden somewhere in my quantum refrigerator is the key to unifying General Relativity and Quantum Mechanics and the secret to finding my way home.

After about another minute of fruitless searching I sigh. Honestly, I'd take some decent food over the secrets to physics at this point. I've just about given up and am picking up the jar of pickles when the doorbell rings. I start at the sudden sound and hit my head. Rubbing my head and cursing, I extricate myself from the refrigerator and walk to the door, wondering who it could be this late.

When I open the door, the first things I see are her eyes. They sparkle warmly in the cool light of the hallway, their color seeming to shift and change like ripples in a river. They're familiar, like I've seen them before; no, not just seen them, but *know* them. Know how they'll shimmer, how their color will flicker now from soft brown to bright green and sparkling blue.

"They're hazel," she says. "I loved them growing up. I couldn't decide which color I liked more. Whenever I had to write my eye color down, I always put brown-green-blue. I only stopped when the DMV refused to put three colors on my driver's license." She laughs and her eyes shimmer, flickering from soft brown to bright green and sparkling blue.

"Hi, sorry for coming by so late," she says.

Her eyes release me then and I see a young woman, a light coat over her cocktail dress and a large paper bag in one hand. A tingling sense of déjà vu lingers over me, and I say the thing—a feeling more than a word—still echoing in my mind: "Ely."

"Jon," she says with a smile.

"The doorman didn't tell me you were coming up," I say slowly, still feeling dazed.

"He recognized me—didn't even have to sign in. I guess I'm one step closer to completing my nefarious plan to break into your apartment and rob you." She winks and then lifts up her paper bag. "I brought you food from the fundraiser. I know how much you love free stuff."

I start to think of an excuse to send her away, remembering that every moment I'm with her I risk forgetting a little more of myself, when my stomach growls hungrily. *I do love free food,* I can't stop myself from thinking.

"Well, are you going to let me in or just stand there starving?" she asks amusedly. Her words are playful, but the blue of her eyes pierces me with their familiarity. They grab onto me and I feel them pulling me in like a river.

I should stay away. She's not real, she's dangerous...

I open my eyes and I'm sitting at my dinner table. Small boxes of food are spread out in front of me and I watch as Ely searches for plates in the kitchen. "I can't believe this is what happens when I leave you alone for a bit," she calls out. "This place is a mess!" My skin prickles and I have a feeling like I've sat here watching her open drawers and cabinets, listening to the clinking sound of plates and silverware, just like this, before. Memories bubble forward and images flash through my mind: her leaning against the kitchen counter laughing, sitting on my couch with the sun in her hair, eyes shimmering as she leans across the table towards me.

They disappear with the clink of a plate and Ely is leaning across the table, pushing a plate of large steamed buns and a pair of chopsticks towards me. "Try these," she says. "They're also vegetarian. Well, everything's vegetarian, but that's the price you pay when you put me in charge of an event."

"Chopsticks, really?" I ask, the words coming on their own. "I'm supposed to eat these with chopsticks?"

"Oh, but that's what you taught me," she replies coyly as she carefully picks up a bun with her chopsticks. "At least that's what I told the mayor. I really hope somebody got a picture of him trying." Her eyes sparkle blue with mischief as she takes a bite, and I can't help but laugh.

I stab a bun with my chopsticks and lift it to my mouth. "That's what you should have done," I say before taking a bite. The bun tastes like home, and when she bursts out laughing it makes me happy.

"So the mayor came to the fundraiser?" I ask, feeling like I already know the answer.

"Oh yes, he was shameless. Gave a big speech about always believing in the Dry Line and being there to show his continued support. After all that funding he cut..."

Her words spark something inside of me and images flash through my mind: water crashing over me as Saniya grabs onto my arm; Saniya running through a street, people and bodies and signs and smoke and chaos all around her; the world twisting and shifting through my tears as the generator's roar floods my ears. Everything's wrong and everywhere is suffering. Except home.

I need to get home.

Ely is leaning towards the flower by my window now. She gently brushes her fingers across the large round leaves and the bulb of the flower and then draws her hand away. "This is beautiful. Where did you get it?"

I look at her and remember her standing there, the sun dancing in her hair as she runs her hands across the flower, and her question feels wrong. "My mom sent it," I say hesitantly, my words also feeling off. "I don't even remember what it is, honestly."

"Is she Buddhist?"

"Yes, how did you know?" I know it doesn't make sense because I've never been here before—never known this girl before tonight—but I can't shake the feeling that this is all wrong: like I'm watching a movie that's not playing out the way it's supposed to.

"This is a lotus," she says as she traces a finger along the edge of the ceramic pot. "It's symbolic in Buddhism." I see her standing by the window with the sunlight streaming around us as she adjusts the flower pot.

"Buddhism teaches that humans are born and reborn into an endless cycle of suffering, rooted in our attachment to the illusion of the permanence of ourselves and the world around us," she says and I'm standing in front of her, her eyes pulling me in again. "A lotus grows out of the mud into a flower. When it opens, it's the promise of escape from the cycle."

The color of her eyes seem to shift and change under the dim light of my apartment, and as they pull me in, it suddenly seems like they are sparkling in sunlight. Like it's a warm summer day and the bright green leaves of Central Park are rustling behind her. "It'll be beautiful when it blooms."

○

The part of me that isn't me feels guilty, but after that night I tell my doorman to not let Ely up anymore and I reply to all her messages that I'm busy. The danger of fake memories alone was enough to want me to keep her away; but there was also something about that night, something about the way my skin tingled and my mind drifted—almost as if I had just run the generator and shifted—that unsettled me.

So I focus on work, and the days pass by in an indistinct blur. Mornings roll into nights into mornings again with only the familiar scrawl of the equations really standing out. I'm vaguely aware of a flurry of events unfolding outside the lab, mostly through Saniya's reports on the mayor's latest outrages: the cuts to education, the "tough on crime" initiatives in the outer boroughs, the feud with Washington over refugee resettlement. Some I half-remember from other shifts and others I'm hearing for the first time. All of them, I ignore. All I need to focus on are my equations. The world might shift and change like a storm-swept river, but the equations are my rock and as long as I hold onto them I'll find my way home.

"So there's a protest planned for the mayor's speech next week."

I look up at Saniya, her words catching my attention in a way they hadn't previously. "You're not thinking of going, are you?"

She sighs. "I know, I know. Scientists shouldn't get involved in politics, it erodes public trust in us. But how can I keep sitting here with my hands under my ass when he's attacking everything we care about?"

"Saniya, no! Please don't." The words burst out of my mouth by themselves, and even I'm surprised at the urgency in them. I don't know why, but I'm overcome by the feeling that I have to stop her.

Saniya seems taken aback as well, and looks at me quietly. "Don't worry," she says after a while. "I've got too much to do right now with your damn equations anyway."

I don't understand the sense of relief that fills me, but my skin continues tingling long after.

○

I'm walking with Saniya through one of the tree-lined, cobblestone paths of the "Square", the small park that connects the malls, museums, and offices that make up the Hudson Yards development. It's a clear, sunny day, but the air is crisp and cool. It's been a long time since I've walked outside like this, and it feels nice.

I stop, feeling like something is wrong. My skin is prickling, as if a cold wave had just washed over me. Saniya looks at me questioningly. "Jon?"

I look back uncertainly. What am I doing here? I feel something in my hand and look down at the paper bag I'm holding. Did we get lunch? There's so much work to do, why would I leave the lab? My mind is buzzing and it almost feels like I've shifted, but...

"Jon!" a familiar voice calls out. It's like the chime of a bell and scatters the questions roiling through my mind. I look up and see Ely ahead of us. Sunlight streams through the trees around her, and when she smiles my skin tingles and it feels like... I struggle to remember the word.

"I thought it was you," she says as she walks up.

"Ely," I say, shifting uneasily. I can feel the fake memories seeping into me, in the way her smile puts me at ease and my mind tells me she's a friend. "What are you doing here?" I ask curtly, pushing all those feelings aside.

Her eyes widen slightly and I know she's taken aback by my coldness. I fight down the feeling of guilt I tell myself isn't real. "Sorry, am I not supposed to be? We did meet here, if you remember."

She's sitting on one of the stone seating walls, the rays of sunlight streaming between the trees seeming to somehow all end with her. She laughs and tries to hold her hair away from her face as it dances in the sudden breeze.

The image fades away and I'm looking into Ely's eyes again. "I was showing some donors the riverfront," she says, breaking the silence I didn't realize had passed. "Helps to give a visual of something before you start begging people for money to fund it. Going to need a lot of that now that the mayor has officially 'completed' the public part of the Dry Line public-private partnership." She rolls her eyes but smiles, and I know she's trying to ease the tension. A part of me wants that too, but another just wants to run away.

Saniya clears her throat loudly and I realize that we've fallen into another awkward silence. "Hi, I'm Saniya," she says, shooting me an annoyed glance before stepping up and offering her hand to Ely.

"I'm Ely," Ely replies as she quickly shakes Saniya's hand. I can sense her relief at Saniya's intervention, and feel another pang of guilt. "Are you friends with Jon?"

"On the good days," Saniya says with a shrug. "Usually I just work with him."

"Oh!" Ely's eyes light up. "Jon's told me about you. You've been friends since college, right?"

Saniya raises an eyebrow and shoots me another glance. "Yes…"

"Well, Jon never told me how gorgeous you are—I love your outfit! You know, we laypeople always imagine scientists running around in white lab coats, but you're just so stylish."

Saniya's face breaks out in a grin and the tension melts away. She's a sucker for compliments. Did I tell Ely that? "Oh, this? It's nothing, I just threw it on this morning. I mean, we actually do wear lab coats at the lab…"

"I mean it. Jon, you're lucky you've had Saniya as a friend all this time. You probably wouldn't have seemed as creepy if she had been with you when we met." She gives me a quick, teasing wink.

"Ohh… I like you!" Saniya gushes. She looks at me, points at Ely a few times and stage whispers loudly, "I really like her!"

Ely laughs and takes Saniya's arm. "Come on, you're at 50 Hudson, right? I'll walk you back."

"It's okay, we can head back ourselves." Even as I say them, the words feel wrong, as if I've lived this moment before and that just wasn't what I was supposed to say.

"Oh shush, you!" Saniya snaps. "Yes Ely, you absolutely must walk us back." She pulls Ely and they start walking together towards the lab.

"It's fine," Ely says to me. "It's close, and besides, I want to hear from Saniya what you were like in college."

Saniya grins. "Oh, you would've hardly recognized him. He was this geeky little kid who didn't have a clue how to talk to real people."

Ely bursts out laughing. "Really? No way!"

"Yes! His sense of humor was the same though, his one redeeming quality..."

I feel my resistance crumbling, as if seeing them meet was the last piece of some puzzle that had been haunting me. I hesitate for a few moments as they walk ahead, and then follow. When I take the first step, it feels like a weight's been lifted; as if I've been swimming against the current of a river and finally decided to let go and drift with it.

As we walk, Ely and Saniya become engrossed in their conversation and seem to forget me. They're relaxed and comfortable, like they've known each other for years, and it feels... right. We walk past a bed of flowers and as a gust of wind picks up, I catch their fragrance in the air. It's soft and delicate, like it would disappear if I breathe too deeply; but it's so familiar, like I've smelled this exact same smell somewhere before. As I breathe in, my skin tingles and a familiar wave washes over me.

The smell comes on a cool summer breeze, soft and delicate like the flowers they come from. I smile, the fragrance lingering in my nose as I watch Ely and Saniya joking and laughing together. I'm glad they're getting along: it's important to me. The wind picks up again and the smell of the flowers drifts away with it.

The scent fades away and the memory with it. I blink a few times, feeling disoriented, like I've just woken up from a dream I'm quickly forgetting; but a part of me is telling me that there's something important about it. *Isn't this the first time they've met?*

"You know, Jon hasn't said anything about you," Saniya's voice cuts in, scattering my thoughts. "I can't believe he's been hiding you."

Ely laughs. "Well, we haven't known each other that long. What's it been Jon, a few months?"

I hesitate. "I think so..."

Ely stops and purses her lips thoughtfully. "No, longer than that I think." She looks at me, and suddenly all I see are her eyes, pulling me in as they shimmer between green and blue under the bright summer sun. "Come on, Jon, don't tell me you've forgotten already?"

*

I'm reviewing calculations from the sensor physics team when I suddenly think of Ely. I don't know why, but one moment I'm cross-checking an equation and the next I remember her eyes sparkling under the sun the day she met Saniya. Didn't I realize something important that day? *When was it?*

At that moment, Saniya opens my door and walks in (she never knocks).

"Hey, what's up?" I ask.

"I missed your face. Seeing it every few hours, 12 hours a day, every day, hasn't been enough for me, so I came here to look at it again." She's impeccably dressed and looks as sharp as always. I would be hard-pressed to tell that she's been in the office every day for the past two weeks working tirelessly.

"Well, look away, take a picture. When you're done, I have work to do." I, on the other hand am particularly feeling the weight of my endless labors today, and probably look like a disheveled mess.

Saniya makes a show of looking me over and then says gravely, "On second thought, this was a bad idea: you look like crap."

I roll my eyes, but she smiles and leans against my table. "Ely and I are going to get lunch at that new Thai place at the Kitchens. Want to come?"

"You've been talking to Ely?" I'm surprised—haven't they just met?

Saniya looks at me strangely. "Um, yes? She's going to become my new best friend, if you don't get your act together. I swear, you care more about this test than me."

"That's not true." I'm doing this for her too. My memories of home are hazy and confused, but I know everything is better there for her too. I struggle to find a memory of her, and a tiny feeling of doubt begins gnawing at me.

"Jon, are you okay?" Saniya's voice cuts through my thoughts. I look up at her worried frown and realize I've been quiet for too long. "You know, you've been really... serious ever since we started working with these new equations."

"I'm fine," I say quickly. "I just want to make sure we're ready for the test." What she said is still bothering me—I know I'm doing this for her too, but I can't seem to remember why.

"Come get lunch with me and Ely."

"You go ahead, I'm in the middle of something." Was it the mayor? Maybe the mayor didn't get re-elected at home?

"Jon, the test will be fine—don't let it take over your life. That was the whole point of us agreeing to work here and building this team, remember?"

"I know, and you know I know that, but this is important. Everything will be fine after the test, I promise." Yes, that must be it. She'd be happy in a world where the mayor was somebody else.

Saniya gives me a long, doubtful look. After a while, she sighs and shrugs. "Okay, fine. I guess you were always either too smart or too lazy to really screw yourself over by overworking."

"Of course, trust me." I force a smile and my words sound more certain than I feel. *Water crashes through the doors, flooding the room, and Saniya screams.*

It's quiet as I walk through the park that runs uptown from the Square past the lab. I follow the soft yellow glow of street-lamps that seem to lead to nowhere, and as the cool night air wraps around me I'm glad I agreed to make this small escape from the lab. I can't remember the last time I've just taken a walk like this.

"Jon?" Her voice drifts to me on the back of a quiet breeze and I look up, not sure if I heard a memory or something real. *I see her walking towards me then, hair rustling quietly in the wind. The moonlight seems to guide her way, and gives her eyes a faint brown-green sparkle. I have a feeling like I'm seeing something from a dream.*

"It is you," Ely says as she steps in front of me. "What are you doing out here?"

"I was... going for a walk," I say slowly, feeling like I've just woken up from a dream—or a memory.

"This late? Did you come from the lab?"

I nod. "I was working and..." Why did I come here? Images flash through my mind. "My mom..." I trail off uncertainly.

"She what? Sent you to your room for being bad?" Ely says with a slight smile.

I relax. That's right actually. Mom had been talking to Saniya again and sent me a flood of messages telling me to stop working so hard before I had a heart attack like Dad. I don't know why I forgot that for a moment, but Ely reminding me is reassuring. I begin lowering the guard I didn't realize I had put up. "Something like that," I say. "She told me to go for a walk first and get connected to nature."

"She sounds great. We'd probably get along—you know me and nature."

I'm not sure I do but nod anyway. "Well, I guess this is about as close to nature as you get in Manhattan," I say as I look around for what feels like the first time. The park feels smaller now and I'm conscious of the buildings rising up around us.

Ely's eyes light up. "Hey, you want to see something amazing?"

I hesitate, but before I can reply she grabs my hand and pulls me with her. "Come on, it's not far. I promise it's worth it."

Her hand feels soft and warm in mine and I instinctively squeeze it to keep it from slipping away. My eyes trace the line of my hand into hers and along her arm to the curve of her shoulder. Moonlight streams down around her and seems to light a path ahead of us. She looks back at me, her eyes a deep ocean blue, and smiles and squeezes my hand back.

She leads us out of the park and we walk quickly through the near-empty streets of West Side Manhattan, talking about nothing and everything: fleeting words quickly forgotten that put me more at ease than I've felt in a long time. We reach the West Side Highway and run across the empty road like kids, her laughter lingering in the night air. She holds my hand the entire way and as I watch the curve of her shoulders rise and fall and the moonlight dance in her hair, my skin tingles and I feel like I'm being pulled into a dream, or perhaps the memory of one.

On the other side of the highway we reach a long metal fence and Ely finally lets go. My empty hand feels cold, and I clench it as I watch her type into a keypad and open a door in the fence. She takes us through into a long park that stretches along the Hudson. I follow her over the grass past scattered trees and up a gentle slope. We sit down at the top and I look down another slope at the Hudson, bathed in moonlight.

"Welcome to the Dry Line," Ely says with a sweeping flourish of her hand. "I can't believe we've known each other this long and I haven't taken you before."

I shift at the reminder that she doesn't really belong in my life, but look around. In a way, the success or failure of the Dry Line determines whether I'm home, but I've never paid it much attention. I see that there's still a lot of work being done: piles of dirt, construction equipment, half-assembled structures, and unplanted trees cover the area. "Where are the flood barriers?" I ask.

"You're sitting on them. The idea was to build something natural that blends into the environment, so you wouldn't notice even if you're right on top of it."

"Like me just now?"

"Exactly." She flashes a satisfied smile. "There are metal locks on the East Side under the FDR, but here we were able to get along with nature a little more. Pretty awesome, right?"

I look down the slope of what I now realize is a long series of hills running along the length of the Hudson. Under the dim glow of the moon, the quietly rustling grass shifts seamlessly into the softly rippling waters of the river. "Yes, it is," I say.

"You know, it barely survived the storm. It wasn't nearly this complete then. So much water got through…" she trails off quietly.

Images flash through my mind: water swallowing up people and bodies floating quietly down flooded avenues. "How bad would it have been?"

"It's hard to say, there are so many variables. The storm weakening, the funding you helped us get… Honestly, I try not to think of it."

I helped her? I'm both surprised and not, and ignore both feelings. "Not at all?" I ask instead.

She laughs softly. "You're just like Saniya—she loves talking about this. She says it's our fault the mayor was re-elected, because he got all the credit for saving the city."

"Maybe it would've been okay." I think of home again. I've taken for granted for so long that everything's better there, but I can't really remember why. It's like an old equation I've forgotten the steps to solving and now all I have is the answer: go home. "Maybe the damage wouldn't have been too bad, and the mayor wouldn't have been re-elected and..." I stop as I realize how obsessive I must sound.

Ely regards me thoughtfully though. After several long moments, she asks, "Have you ever been to a forest, Jon?"

"Does Central Park count?" I feel like I want to see her smile again and somehow know she'll like this joke.

She rolls her eyes but smiles slightly and I relax. "You're such a city boy—I'll have to take you to a real forest sometime. The Catskills are nice. We should go there, if you really want to get connected to nature."

My skin tingles but no images flash through my mind. It's just a feeling like I've lived this moment before.

"Sometimes when I'm there I just sit and listen to the wind and the birds, and it feels like... everything is connected. Like even though I'm trying to stay still, the world keeps moving and I'm not supposed to fight it." She looks at me and her eyes glimmer a deep brown under the pale moonlight. "Nothing is permanent, Jon. Not what's happening now and certainly not what might have been. The world is always moving. The only way we can really stay still is to live in each moment and move with it."

She turns back towards the river and looks into it quietly. I follow her gaze and begin to barely make out the ripples of the waters' ebbs and flows under the dim glow of the moon. I think I can almost see myself in them.

*

As I get closer to completing the calculations, the days begin to feel strangely disjointed. I don't know why, but each one feels somehow disconnected from the next, as if every morning I'm stepping from one life into another. It's a feeling that possesses me more and more every day: a hazy, lingering, uncertainty that leaves my skin tingling. I know I have a word for it, but it keeps slipping my mind. The only things that feel clear are my equations, and I throw myself into them, taking comfort in their familiarity. I'm being tossed around in a constantly shifting river, the currents pulling me under, and they're my rock. One day I begin to lose even that.

"This isn't right!" I shout again, slamming my hands on the table in frustration.

The team leaders around me in the main lab flinch. They're not used to seeing me like this, and are uncomfortable, but I don't care. I just glare at the rows of equations and calculations on the digital board that I *know* are wrong.

Saniya also doesn't care. She spins me around by my shoulder and pins me with a cold stare. "Dammit, Jon, get a grip of yourself. We've been going over this all day. They're *right* and they're based on *your* equations."

I understand logically what she's saying. The math makes sense and we went through the work logs all the way back to the beginning to make sure. But I also know, as surely as I know my name, that it can't be right—the team *must* have messed up somewhere—because when I combine our work to calculate the coil configuration for the next test, I get the exact same one I used for my last shift. It was, in effect, telling me I'm already home.

"Jon," Saniya says, more gently this time. "Are you alright?"

"It doesn't make sense..." I sigh. If it was just close, maybe I could explain it, but the exact same configuration? It's impossible...

"Alright, everybody take the rest of the day off!" Saniya says suddenly. An uneasy murmur starts that she quickly cuts off. "You heard me! Life is short, get out of here and do something meaningful with it."

The others clear the lab quietly after that, though I catch a few sidelong glances. Saniya waits until they're all gone, and then looks at me worriedly. "Seriously Jon, what's going on? You know the calculations are right. Since when did you start trusting your math over mine, anyway?"

I look back at the board. She's right, and yet... "I'm sorry Saniya, just... give me some time." To convince myself that I'm wrong and not the world? It goes against everything I've learned from countless shifts.

"Why don't you take the day off too? Give Ely a call, take her to dinner."

"Ely? Why?" I don't even remember the last time I saw her, much less how she could help.

"Don't be an asshole to her too, okay? At least I know when you're not being yourself." Saniya gives me a look like she's scolding a child. "Anyway, if you're really going to spend all day confirming my work's better than yours, then I'm going to go see the mayor's speech with some non-crazy friends."

I feel a surge of fear. "You're going to a protest?"

"Protest? Why would I protest New York's first female mayor? We're going to celebrate!"

I stare at where Saniya had been for a while after she leaves. What she said feels wrong too, but for the life of me I can't remember why.

◌

The elevator doors open and I step wearily out into the lobby. I worked all afternoon and feel more tired and less sure of myself than when I started. Saniya was right—everything made sense: her math, the equations, everything—and I still know that isn't possible. I hesitate as a thought I've been avoiding sneaks up on me again: *Could I be remembering something wrong?*

A loud alarm screeches from my phone and I pull it out of my pocket in annoyance. As I look at the message on the screen, my skin tingles with electricity and a familiar wave pulls me in.

I read the message on my phone: "EMERGENCY ALERT. Mandatory evacuation in effect in Manhattan. Go to nearest evacuation point immediately."

I hear a loud splash and look up to see Saniya stumble out of the emergency stairwell into the knee-deep water that's flooded the lobby. I'm so relieved to see her that I forget for a moment the storm raging just outside. "Saniya!" I shout.

She looks at me in surprise. "Jon? What the hell are you doing here?"

"Looking for you, you idiot! What are you still doing here—we have to get out of the city now!"

I step forward and my feet sinks into the cold water with a splash. I look around the suddenly dark and empty lobby in confusion; outside I hear the angry howling of a storm. I look down at the phone still in my hand and read the message: "EMERGENCY ALERT. FLOODING IMMINENT. SEEK HIGH GROUND IMMEDIATELY."

Where am I? Wasn't I just in the elevator?

"Jon!" Someone grabs me by my shoulder and I turn to see Saniya. "You saw the message, get back upstairs!" She pushes me towards the stairwell and starts wading through the water towards the entrance.

"Where are you going?" I shout after her.

"To get my grandmother! She lives in a walk-up and still writes me letters!"

I wrap one arm around the pole as the water crashes angrily over us. My other hand clings desperately to Saniya's, trying to pull her closer to me even as the water tears us apart. I want to look back at her, to find her face and tell her to hold on, but the water blinds me and I feel her fingers slowly slip out of mine. "Jon!" she shouts, though I barely hear her over the storm and water. "Just let—"

"Saniya, no!" I start to rush after her, and am blinded by smoke. I fall to my knees on what feels like rough asphalt, coughing and suddenly aware of the screaming and shouting surrounding me. Shadowy figures, half-hidden in the smoke, run all around me. Shots ring out and I hear sirens echoing in the distance. My skin is tingling and my mind feels heavy, almost as if I had just shifted.

"Jon..." a voice rasps out. I feel a hand brush weakly against mine and instinctively take it. *This... this is...* The smoke clears slightly, and I see Saniya lying on the ground, a jagged flower of blood blooming across her chest.

"Saniya, no, no..." I mutter, a numbing fear rising up inside me. *This happened before...* It doesn't make sense, but some part of me is telling me that this happened before and I'll make it okay, I'll fix it and we'll go home. "I'll fix it, don't worry I'll fix it. It's all in the equations. I'll fix it and we're going to go home..." I repeat the words desperately. I don't know what they mean, only that they have to be right.

Saniya smiles faintly up at me. "It's okay, Jon..." she murmurs. "It's okay... just let go..." I can't see her anymore through the smoke and the tears stinging my eyes, and the generator's roar floods my ears.

○

I open my eyes, feeling confused and disoriented. What am I doing? There's something I'm supposed to do... "My name is Jon, I'm a physicist," I say, becoming aware now that I'm sitting by a table. The words are familiar and comforting, and I cling onto them as I try to shake off the disorientation that always comes after a test.

No, that's not right... "My name is Jon," I say again. There hasn't been a test yet. I've... what have I been doing? "My name is Jon, I'm—"

"Did you forget your name, Jonathan S. Lee?"

The voice—light, playful, and *familiar*—cuts through my daze and I turn towards it. I see Ely leaning towards a window. Sunlight streams through it, falling all around her, bathing my apartment with a soft, white glow.

Jonathan. That's right. I can't remember the last time somebody called me that, but that's me and I'm with Ely in my apartment. I'm sitting by my dinner table, and there's an open jar of pickles near my hand. Everything seems to be in its place, and Mom's Buddha statue contemplates me nearby. Slowly, the fog around my mind begins to drift away.

Ely is adjusting a white ceramic bowl by the window. Long green stems shoot up out of it, most of them ending in large roundish leaves; the tallest stem though thrusts above the leaves and ends in the slender red bulb of a flower. After a few moments, Ely stops and nods. She turns to look at me, her eyes shimmering green in the sunlight and the bright green leaves of Central Park rustling behind her.

"It's a lotus flower," she says. "It should bloom by the end of summer if you manage not to kill it first. I think even you'll be okay with this one though—it's super easy to take care of. You just need to keep the water level right, and then just let it grow." She gently brushes her fingers across the large round leaves and the bulb of the flower before drawing her hand away.

"You got this for me?" I ask. The question feels important.

"Well, it was your mom's idea, but I'll take some credit too. She ordered me around and I listened to her." She laughs softly and walks over to me. As she looks at me her eyes draw me in with the way they seem to shimmer and shift between all their colors. "I think it's going to bloom soon," she says as she sits down and takes my hands in hers. They're warm and familiar and I squeeze them instinctively. "It'll be beautiful when it does."

Her words are the first things that feel right to me in a long time.

I'm staring through the reinforced glass windows at the end of the generator control room. A steady electric hum emanates from the chamber on the other side and I watch as the eight cavorite columns inside shift and rotate into the positions I calculated: the configuration that would...

I blink a few times, feeling disoriented. I look around and see Saniya next to me in front of the main control panel and the rest of the team positioned at the various monitoring stations. *What am I doing here?*

"Test configuration set," Saniya says as the coils lock into place with loud, hissing snaps. She shakes her head. "You're going to have to explain to me again later why we're using this completely random configuration for our first test."

That's right, I finally figured out what was wrong with the calculations... right?

"Beginning warm-up cycle," Saniya says. She taps on the screen of her panel and the coils inside the chamber light up and the electric hum grows louder.

I can't help but feel like I'm missing something, but I'm not sure what. The flashes have cone more frequently lately: real and fake memories swirling confusingly together, so vivid they often seem to spill into reality. They make sense and they don't and sometimes I wonder if they ever really ended or if I'm still stumbling through a memory now... This should terrify me, but...

Nothing is permanent, Jon. Not what's happening now and certainly not what might have been.

Who had said that? Somebody I knew? Somebody important to me...

A loud beep scatters my thoughts and I see the chamber again. "Warm-up cycle complete," Saniya announces. "All stations confirm systems green." She turns and looks at me expectantly. "Are you ready, Jon?"

I hesitate, not sure what I'm supposed to do. After a few moments, I nod. "Start the generator."

Home. I'm supposed to go home.

"Activating the generator," Saniya says as she taps her screen. The hum of electricity grows louder as power courses through the coils. The laser sensor array blankets the generator chamber in angry red beams and a murmur of excitement ripples through the team.

Not much longer now. My thoughts are still scattered, and I press my hands against the cold metal of the control panel, focusing on how it feels.

Her hand feels soft and warm in mine and I instinctively squeeze it to keep it from slipping away. My eyes follow the line of my hand into hers and along her arm to the curve of her shoulder. Sunlight dances in her hair and I breathe in the fresh scent of pine and early morning dew. Rays of sunlight burst between the leaves of the trees, piercing the forest canopy with lances of light, and seeming to light a path ahead of us. She looks back at me, her eyes a brilliant sky blue, and smiles and squeezes my hand back.

The electric hum of the coils is louder now. I reach for her hand and feel only cold metal. Everything seems distant and I'm not sure where I am, but the scent of pine lingers in the air. A forest... didn't she say she'd take me to one? But she didn't—not yet. None of this makes sense...

"Huh, I just had the weirdest feeling..." Saniya says, and her voice draws me back to the room, to the generator. Yes, the generator, that's where I am.

"What... did you say?" I stammer, feeling like I've just woken up.

"I just had a feeling like we've done this before. Like I was standing right here with you watching this happen before. It feels like..."

Déjà vu. That was the word. That was the word I'd forgotten.

The room seems to spin around me and a thousand images from a thousand lives flash before me. Saniya: lying in the street, dying in the street; slipping into the water, pulling me from it; laying her grandmother down; sobbing at Battery Park, tears of joy running down her cheeks. Ely: a park, a forest, a roof, my room, my arms around her, her arms around me, and her eyes—always shifting, never changing: her eyes. And me: in the lab, in my apartment, the city flooding outside and covered in smoke and fire, pouring over the equations—always shifting, never changing: the equations.

I see them as they really are: memories of pasts yet to be, futures already come, and everything in between—all connected. I'm sitting with Ely on the unfinished banks of a river and see my life and all those moments rushing by in the water: ebbs and flows, ripples and whirls that split and mingle and change each other, moving forwards and backwards all at once before finally joining together again.

The world is always moving. The only way we can really stay still is to live in each moment and move with it. All this time I thought the generator—*I thought I*—was the only one shifting the world; but I finally realize now what all the flashes and disjointed memories I've been experiencing mean. Perhaps it was the generator and the endless shifts it sent me through that allowed me to finally see it, but the world is always shifting and changing too, and when it does... if it touches you, it feels like déjà vu.

I see the generator now, hear its electric hum echoing loudly through the room. I know where I am and what to do: I have to escape the cycle. I have to stop fighting and surrender myself to the river. I have to accept where the world wants me to go.

"Saniya, stop the test."

"What did you say?"

"Stop the test!"

"Are you crazy?! Why?" she looks at me eyes wide in disbelief.

"Saniya please just trust me, we have to stop the test now!" I summon every bit of pleading, urgency, desperation, sincerity, and truth I can muster—across a thousand lifetimes of friendship—as I look into her eyes.

She hesitates for only a few moments longer before turning to the control panel. "God damn men…" she says loudly as she taps the screen. Minutes pass and her tapping continues, becoming gradually more urgent; but the hum of the generator seems to only get louder. Finally, she stops and looks up, a panicked look on her face. "It's not stopping!"

"What do you mean? Did you manually cut the power?"

"Of course I did! But the coils are still active! Gravitational distortions are getting stronger!" Saniya begins shouting orders at the team and I feel fear rippling through the room. The humming of the coils turns into a roar, and I can barely hear myself think. As the sound grows even louder, I see the red beams of the sensor array begin to distort, slowly twisting like they're caught in a whirlpool.

"Jon! Do you see this?" Saniya exclaims.

The sound of the generator becomes thunderous and everything around me begins to twist and warp. I begin to feel like all I'm really seeing is a faint impression of some forgotten memory. The coils, the chamber, my hands on the panel—they all seem so indistinct, like they aren't really there.

A hand grabs onto mine and I turn to see Saniya, eyes wide and fear etched across her slowly twisting face. I remember her lying on the street, blood spreading across her chest like a red flower and fear rising in mine.

"It's okay, Saniya." I squeeze her hand back. "It's okay, just let—"

I feel then like *I'm* twisting, my body being pulled in all directions and back again at once. And then the noise is gone and everything is dark. I can't feel Saniya's hand or my own and the only thing I hear is the echo of a familiar voice, telling me things I wanted to say.

I walk through the Square, hugging the large brown take-out bag in my arms. I asked Saniya to get lunch with me, but she's been wanting to spend most of her time in the lab lately; so I offered to pick something up for her, which quickly escalated into buying burritos for the rest of the team. Ah, the duties of a co-director...

Well, if that means Saniya's stuck in the lab checking my calculations while I enjoy this lovely summer day, who am I to complain?

Something catches my eyes and I stop. I'm not sure what it is but I turn and look to my side. I see her then, sitting on one of the stone seating walls, the rays of sunlight streaming between the trees seeming to somehow all end with her.

She's reading a book, and something draws me to her. I'm not the type of person to approach strangers in a park (that's more Saniya's thing) but I lower my bag of burritos and walk up to her. "Hello," I try.

She looks up at me and I'm struck by the way her eyes seem to shimmer and shift colors as she moves. "Hi," she says, giving me a not-unfriendly smile.

I hesitate, not sure what I'm doing or what to say, when it suddenly comes to me. "Do you work at the Dry Line?"

She glances down at the folders by her side, held down against the wind by a small jar of pickles and marked in large block letters: DRY LINE WEST SIDE COASTAL RESILIENCY PROJECT. "How did you guess that?" she asks, her lips quirking slightly.

I shift uncomfortably. "Ah, I mean…" This is not going how I expected. What had I expected? "Do you need help with it?" I blurt out.

She purses her lips and gives me a curious look. "You know, that actually might be one of the better pick-up lines I've heard. Not that that's saying much—they're all pretty bad."

I feel my face heating up. "That's not what I'm doing! It's a really important project and I want to help…"

She laughs and lifts a hand up to hold her hair away from her face as it dances in a sudden gust of wind. "I'm sorry," she says, seeming embarrassed herself now. "That's really nice of you."

"I really do want to help," I say again lamely.

Her face becomes thoughtful and she regards me quietly. As she looks at me, her eyes draw me in. They sparkle warmly in the light of the summer sun, their color seeming to shift and change like ripples in a river. They're so familiar, like I've seen them before; no, not just seen them, but *know* them. Know how they'll shimmer, how their color will flicker now from soft brown to bright green and sparkling blue.

"Sorry," she says after what feels like a long time. "I just had the strangest feeling that we've met before."

I continue looking at her quietly for a few moments more and then hold out my hand. "I'm Jonathan."

She puts her book down and shakes my hand. There's something warm and familiar about her touch.

"I'm Elysia," she says. "But my friends call me Ely."

"Elysia?" I feel like I've just remembered something I'd forgotten.

"It means home." She smiles and her eyes seem to settle onto a light blue that reflects the sky. I see myself in them.

Phong Quan's story "It Feels Like Déjà Vu" was first published in Metaphorosis *on 27 July 2018.*

About the author

Phong's parents are from tropical Vietnam, so after they immigrated to the United States of course he was born in Minnesota on April 1 st , the last day of a big snow storm—a great April Fool's joke for everyone involved. Immediately afterwards, his family moved to sunny California where he was raised. He eventually became a corporate lawyer and has worked in New York, Beijing and Singapore, where he is currently based.

A House on the Volga

Filip Wiltgren

The kalanchoes are blooming, a dusting of tiny pink flowers on dark jade leaves.

"Please, grandmama, hurry up," says Darius, voice tiny, his heart carried on the radio from the ship.

He is a good boy, caring for his grandmother. His heart was in his house, but he is grown, a young man, and the house is no more. It is good that he leave.

The kalanchoe spins in my hands, as I cover it in plastic, round and round, like a tiny asteroid around a distant sun, pink flowers turning.

Darius' voice is tiny as a single flower.

"Atmospheric impact in twelve minutes," he says, hints of panic in his voice.

"I know," I say. My hands are clumsy around the kalanchoes, wet soil crumbling from wet pots, seen through wet eyes. It is not good, being last.

Our asteroid has lost internal gravity. In twelve minutes it will lose everything. I keep wrapping kalanchoes in plastic. Six foil-wrapped bundles float by my side, another ten sit on their perches in our dorm. My dorm, now.

"We built this together, your grandfather and I," I tell Darius. "Our home, and yours, too."

"I know, grandmama. Please hurry."

"I will," I say. Seven floating bundles. Impact in eleven minutes.

"Mother, what do you think you are doing?" Michail's voice comes strong and loud. No tiny suit microphone for him, the big engineer.

"Engineer Litvinenko, I presume?" I ask, as chilly as I can. His voice continues uninterrupted. For two hours, it has flown. From his office on the Moon, to the Volga's orbit around Saturn. Michail's grand office, where he's making a name for himself, ignoring his house. Selling it.

"- the GN/BN-22 is company property, mother. You return it to regular orbit right this minute, you hear? The lawyers will-"

"Czernobog take the lawyers."

And this asteroid has always been the House by the Volga. GN/BN is a designation. The Volga is a home. Michail never understood that.

Nine bundles by my side. Seven kalanchoes to go. A single detached, pink flower floats by, like a heart without a home.

Vladek brought our first kalanchoe shoot with him when we moved up, and they've grown well. Flowers thrive when there's love in the house.

For a moment I can hear Vladek's voice, but then I only hear the memory of escaping air, and the snap of radio static. So much lost to the stars. So much pain, so many memories. In the end, everything dies, this is the way of life. But as long as the hearts are beating, the family will remember. That is the way of life, too.

A warning shrieks. The system is trying to override.

Michail. Trying to control what cannot be controlled, take back what wasn't given.

I yank out a circuit board, then reset the course computer.

"Grandmama, you need to flee."

"Soon," I tell Darius.

"Now, grandmama!"

Two kalanchoes left. I bundle the first one. Five minutes. Fifteen kalanchoes float tightly in my arms, then float freely as I release them into an escape pod before strapping them down in the only remaining seat. Every birth, every marriage, we planted a new one, a flash of flowers in the dormitory. When the hearts left, we kept the flowers as memories.

Children, grandchildren, everyone has left the Volga. Even Vladek is gone, lost to the void. Perhaps it was stupid to give Michail power of attorney. He never understood how much we struggled to make a home after the exodus. You can no more abandon your home than abandon your heart, or your family.

"Darius," I say. "are you ready for pick-up?"

"God be blessed, grandmama. Plotting intercept now."

"Take care of our flowers," I say, closing the pod door.

The airlock cycles. The pod launches.

"Grandmama?"

The panic is back in Darius' voice. He is a good boy. He will understand, I think. I shut down the radio, severing the cables, and the possibility of a remote redirection of the Volga.

The family is gone, the House by the Volga sold, to be melted down for the nickel in its shell. But a house full of love is like a member of your family, and you do not abandon family. You follow them to their grave, and then you bury them. I take the last kalanchoe in my arms.

Vladek's flower. The original one. He wanted to give it to me, but I said no. He had brought it from Earth. It was his heart.

I kiss the flower, its leaves smooth against my coarse, chapped lips.

"Goodbye, you old heart breaker," I say, "hold a seat in heaven for me."

Then I replace the kalanchoe on its perch and push off toward the last escape pod. The airlock cycles, the acceleration slams me into the grav-couch. Darius' voice comes tiny over the pod's speakers.

"Grandmama!" he says, relief saturating his tones, "for a moment I thought..."

A sad smile crosses my lips.

"You are family," I say.

"But the Volga—"

"Will be buried," I say. Then I shut off the radio, and watch a home briefly bloom against the great globe of Saturn.

Filip Wiltgren's story "A House on the Volga" was first published in Metaphorosis *on 9 November 2018.*

About the author

By day, Filip Wiltgren is a mild-mannered communication officer at Linköping University, where he also teaches communication and presentation skills at a post-graduate level. But by night, he turns into a frenzied ten-fingered typist, clawing out jagged stories of fantasy and science fiction, which have found lairs in places such as Analog, Grimdark, Daily SF, and Nature Futures. Filip roams the Swedish highlands, kept in check by his wife and kids. He can be found at www.wiltgren.com

Copyright

First appearance

All stories first appeared in *Metaphorosis,* except

"Pandora, Rising" first appeared in *Galaxy's Edge*
"Replica" first appeared in *Abyss and Apex*
"Elegy of Carbon" first appeared in *The Internet Is Where the Robots Live Now*
"A Cigarette Burn on Your Memory" first appeared in *Clarkesworld*
"In All Possible Futures" first appeared in *Future SF*
"Last Contact" first appeared in *Nature*

Metaphorosis Publishing

Metaphorosis offers beautifully written science fiction and fantasy. Our imprints include:

Metaphorosis Magazine

Plant Based Press

Metaphorosis Books

Driftwyrd

Vestige

See more about some of our books on the following pages.

Metaphorosis
a magazine of speculative fiction

Metaphorosis is a weekly science fiction and fantasy magazine. Find out more at magazine.metaphorosis.com, and sign up to be notified when new stories come out every Friday.

We also publish monthly print and e-book issues, as well as yearly Best of and Complete anthologies.

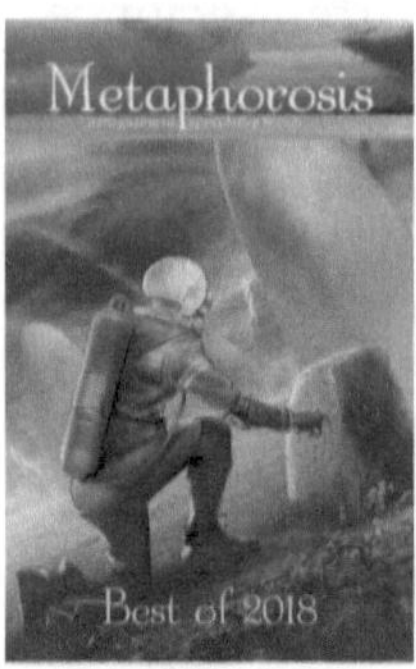

**Metaphorosis:
Best of 2018**

The best science fiction and fantasy stories from *Metaphorosis* magazine's third year.

Metaphorosis 2018

All the stories from *Metaphorosis* magazine's third year. Fifty-two great SFF stories.

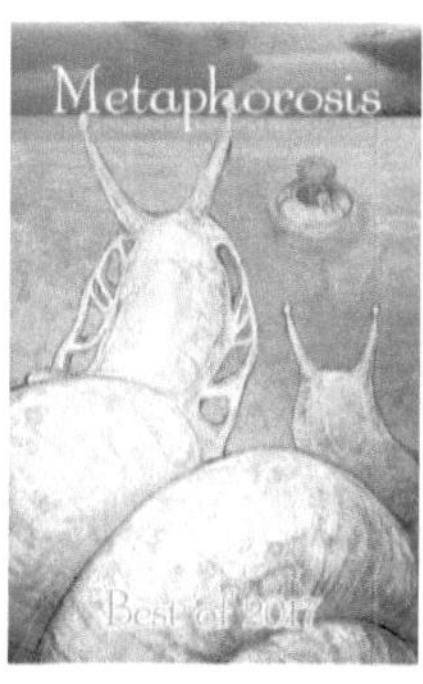

Metaphorosis:
Best of 2017

The best science fiction and fantasy stories from *Metaphorosis* magazine's *second* year.

Metaphorosis 2017

All the stories from *Metaphorosis* magazine's second year. Fifty-three great SFF stories.

Metaphorosis:
Best of 2016

The best science fiction and fantasy stories from *Metaphorosis* magazine's first year.

Metaphorosis 2016

Almost all the stories from *Metaphorosis* magazine's first year.

Plant Based Press

Vegan-friendly science fiction and fantasy, including an annual anthology of the year's best SFF stories.

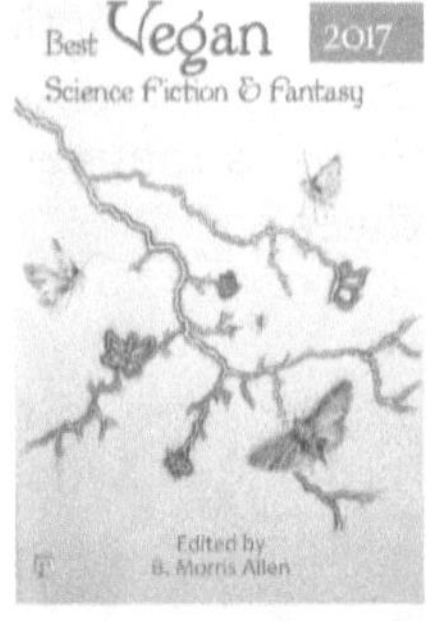

**Best Vegan SFF
of 2018**

**Best Vegan SFF
of 2017**

The best vegan science fiction and fantasy stories of 2018!

The best vegan science fiction and fantasy stories of 2017!

Best Vegan SFF
of 2016

The best vegan science fiction and fantasy stories of 2016!

Susurrus

A darkly romantic story of magic, love, and suffering.

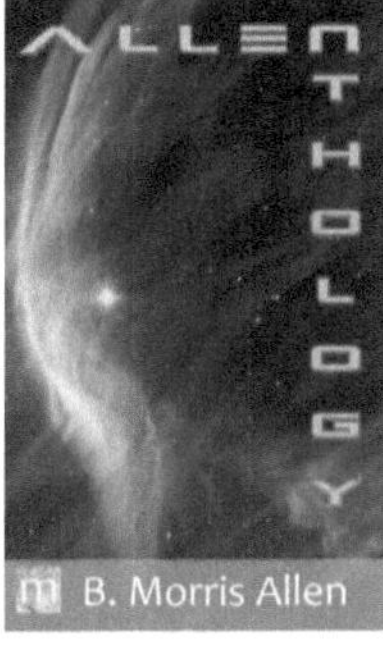

Allenthology: Volume I

A quarter century of SFF stories, including the full contents of the collections *Tocsin, Start with Stones,* and *Metaphorosis.*

Metaphorosis Books

Science fiction and fantasy books for writers – full of great stories, but with an additional focus on the craft of speculative fiction writing.

Score

an SFF symphony

What if stories were written like music? *Score* is an anthology of varied stories arranged to follow an emotional score from the heights of joy to the depths of despair – but always with a little hope shining through.

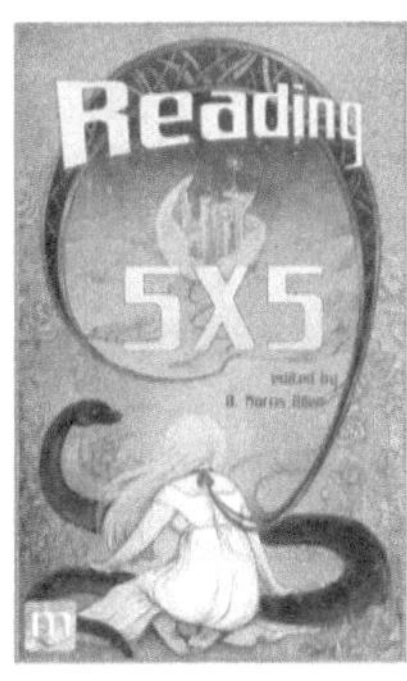

Reading 5X5

Five stories, five times

Twenty-five SFF authors, five base stories, five versions of each – see how different writers take on the same material, with stories in contemporary and high fantasy, soft and hard SF, and a mysterious 'other' category.

Reading 5X5

Writers' Edition

All the stories from the regular, readers' edition, plus two extra stories, the story seed, and authors' notes on writing. Over 100 pages of additional material specifically aimed at writers.

www.ingramcontent.com/pod-product-compliance
Lightning Source LLC
Chambersburg PA
CBHW020326110726
47898CB00003B/763